"I'll thaw out in a minute,"
Emmy said, her voice muffled.
"How about you?"

"I'm fine where I am, too."

At Jack's quiet admission, Emmy felt the tightness in her chest loosen a little more. It seemed easier to breathe when he held her. She had no idea why that was but she wouldn't question it now. Now, she wanted simply to...be.

"Jack?"

"Yeah?"

Beneath her ear she could hear the strong rhythm of his heart. Placing her palm over that steady beat, she moved closer to absorb the warmth seeping into her from his arms. "I'm going to miss you."

The beat didn't change, but his voice seemed to drop as he smoothed his hand the length of her ponytail.

"I guess that makes us even."

The Sugar House
CHRISTINE FLYNN

SILHOUETTE®

SPECIAL EDITION™

Silhouette, Silhouette Special Edition and Colophon are registered
trademarks of Harlequin Books S.A., used under licence.

First published in Great Britain 2006
Silhouette Books, Eton House, 18-24 Paradise Road,
Richmond, Surrey TW9 1SR

© Christine Flynn 2005

ISBN 0 373 24690 0

23-0606

Printed and bound in Spain
by Litografia Rosés S.A., Barcelona

CHRISTINE FLYNN

admits to being interested in just about everything, which is why she considers herself fortunate to have turned her interest in writing into a career. She feels that a writer gets to explore it all and, to her, exploring relationships—especially the intense, bittersweet or even lighthearted relationships between men and women—is fascinating.

To my lovely niece, Elizabeth Weckstein.
You are a young woman of amazing potential.
Don't ever forget how special you are.
Much love, Auntie Chris

Chapter One

She shouldn't have answered the telephone, Emmy Larkin thought. She should have grabbed her parka and headed out into the glorious winter sunshine as she'd started to do, and let the thing ring. Now she knew for certain that the disturbing rumors were true.

"I tell you, I just saw him myself, Emmy. I was in front of the store helping Mary Moorehouse load her groceries when this black car with New York plates came up Main. New York is where he lives now, you know," Agnes Waters confided over the line. "My cousin at the county recorder's office in St. Johnsbury saw his address when she recorded the deed selling that property to him.

"Anyway," the chatty owner of Maple Mountain's quaint old general store continued, anxious to share her news, "you know we don't get many strangers here this time of year, so the car had me paying particular attention. There's no doubt in my mind it was him. I told Mary the second I realized it for sure that I had to let poor Emmy know that Jack Travers is here."

Poor Emmy.

Emmy flinched at the label. It was the woman's news, however, that robbed the usual smile from her voice. "I appreciate you thinking of me, Agnes."

"Well, of course I'd think of you." The insistence in the older woman's tone made it sound as if she'd just planted her fist on one rather ample hip. "After what his father did to yours, I think it's an insult to you that he'd even show his face around here. After all those fights he got himself into, I can't imagine why he'd want to come back here at all.

"As for him buying that property," she continued, her indignation mounting, "I tell you there's not a member of the community council that's going to sit by and let him build fancy condos or whatever he has in mind on those ten acres. I don't believe for a minute that he's just building himself a vacation house. I know Mary said that was always a possibility, but I can't imagine why he'd think he or any member of his family would ever be welcome here."

Stretching the long phone cord as far as it would go, Emmy tugged her heavy blue parka from its hook by her sugar house's door. She had heard talk about Jack Travers for nearly two weeks. Every time she walked into the post office, the community center or the Waters's store with its pot-bellied stove and creaky wooden floors, people would be buzzing about him buying the property or rehashing what his dad had done to hers. The instant they noticed her, though, a sympathetic and speculative silence inevitably fell.

She was twenty-seven years old and, still, no one wanted to talk in front of her about how Ed Travers had harmed her father's ability to make a living. Or about how it might not have been an accident that a few years later her father had lost control of his car and run head-on into a tree. Or, about how her mom had never been the same after his death and simply wasted away, leaving Emmy all alone.

The acreage Jack had bought had once belonged to her father. The maple-tree-covered land had been part of the sugar bush her dad had carefully tended for its sap, and was the parcel he'd used to secure a loan from Jack's father to buy new sugaring equipment. Her dad hadn't been able to pay the money back when it was due, though. And Ed Travers hadn't been willing to give his long-time friend even a few months longer to repay it. He'd filed for foreclosure on the property and ultimately sold it to an outsider for far less than it had been worth.

Jack's father had recovered his money, but her father and his business had been devastated. Without those trees, the income from the maple sugaring operation that had helped support his family had been cut by a third.

Emmy knew the only reason Agnes had alluded to what had happened now was because she'd wanted to warn her that the man's son was there. The silence on the other end of the line seemed to indicate that she was also waiting for her to say something that would at least vindicate the urgency she'd felt to get to the phone with her news. Or perhaps something she could share with whoever happened to walk in next to the only place for miles where a person could get everything from sporting gear to butter and eggs.

Like almost everyone in the rural and isolated community of Maple Mountain, Vermont, Agnes had a good heart. And like everyone else who lived on the outlying farms and in the rolling, wooded hills, she wasn't terribly tolerant of anyone who tried to change their ways or their attitudes or who threatened one of their own. For all their independence, they looked out for each other. And for many, like Agnes, minding everyone's business wasn't regarded so much as a sport as it was a sacred duty.

"I guess we'll just have to wait and see what he has in mind," Emmy finally replied, practical as always. "But I can't imagine he'd feel welcome here, either."

Like Agnes, she couldn't imagine why he had bought the property adjacent to hers. The tree-dense parcel had passed from one out-of-state owner to another over the past fifteen years. Some investor or professional couple from down country would buy it with grandiose plans for its development, then figure out how impractical those plans were, leave it as it was, and put it back on the market. Invariably, the property sat for sale for a couple of years before someone else would come along and start the cycle all over again.

Jack Travers wasn't like those other buyers, though. He'd been familiar with that land. He knew its rolling terrain. He had to know exactly what he'd bought. As a teenager he'd worked it with her father.

Trying to ignore the odd sense of apprehension the conversation brought, she pulled on her jacket while holding the phone between her shoulder and chin. As she did, Rudy, her fifty-pounds of energetic retriever mixed with mutt leaped from his bed under her desk and planted his golden-haired body by the door. He sat there vibrating, dark eyes bright.

"I'm sorry, Agnes." Now that her parka was on, she reached for her gray fleece cap. "I'm going to have to run. I was just on my way to the house to bring something back for supper before my next batch of sap starts to boil." She moved toward the receiver on the desk at the back of the room, pulling gloves from her jacket pocket on the way. She didn't know when she'd have another break before darkness fell. She didn't mind making the trip to the house in the dark. It was just easier with daylight. "Before I forget," she hurried to say, "you mentioned that you'd helped Mary with her groceries. Did she say how Charlie is doing?"

"His gout is about the same." If Agnes was disappointed by her lack of verbal reaction to Jack's presence, she didn't let on. Emmy knew she'd been concerned about Charlie, too. "He still can't get on a boot."

"He's probably going stir crazy not being able to get out of the house."

Agnes gave an unladylike snort. "Don't know about him. But he's sure making Mary that way."

A faint smile entered Emmy's voice. "I imagine he is." As cantankerous as her old friend and part-time employee could be on a good day, he'd be like a bear with a toothache on a bad one. "Thanks for calling, Agnes. I really appreciate it. You take care. Okay?"

Emmy didn't want to be rude. But she really didn't have long before she had to get back to work. Boiling maple sap into syrup sounded simple enough, but the chores involved would keep her there until midnight.

Agnes took no offense at all at being rushed off the phone. Like every other local, she knew that when sugar season came, the flow of the sap dictated the course of the day for anyone with a sugaring operation. Since Agnes also knew that Emmy was working alone because Charlie, her only help, was temporarily out of commission, she was off the phone in the time it took her to tell Emmy she'd let her know if she heard anything about Jack that Emmy needed to be concerned about.

Emmy had barely replaced the receiver of the old black dial phone when Rudy started turning circles by the door, anxious to get out.

It was such a little thing, but at that moment, Emmy could have hugged him for his predictability. Had he not just started spinning, she would have. So much about her life had been unexpected. So many things had happened that she hadn't been able to see coming. Having been blind-sided so often, she'd grown to love routine, thought of *change* as a four-letter word, and adored anything predict-able. If Rudy was anything, he was a creature of habit, and she loved him for that.

Pulling her hat over her stick-straight auburn ponytail, she smiled at the blur of circling fur and opened the door of the small weather-grayed building before he could make himself dizzy.

Cold air rushed into the warm, sweet-smelling space as Rudy bolted out. With his nose to the foot-deep snow, he ran, sniffing, to see what sort of critter had invaded his turf since he'd last patrolled his domain.

Emmy followed more slowly, taking the path through the trees that led to her yard, her snow-covered garden and her back porch. Depending on how much snow the front predicted to move in tomorrow brought, in another few weeks, she might even see bare ground. That meant mud and rain, but it also meant crocus and daffodils and buds on the trees.

Trying to think of simple, ordinary things, things she loved and looked forward to, wasn't working.

The sense of foreboding wouldn't go away.

She couldn't imagine why Jack had come back. It was beyond her comprehension why any Travers would want anything at all to do with a place where the mere mention of their family name conjured tales of disloyalty, greed and poor Stan Larkin and his little family.

Poor Stan Larkin. Poor Emmy. Her poor mother.

She mentally cringed every time she heard the word that labeled them all so unfortunate and pitiable. Being the subject of talk had always made her uneasy. Being the subject of pity made her even more so. She was equally uncomfortable with the sympathetic looks and the well-intentioned comments she'd heard lately about how well she was taking "the news." But she hadn't dealt with the news as well as she'd let on.

Snow crunched beneath her feet as she watched Rudy eye an unsuspecting squirrel. It had taken her forever to get past the feeling that at any moment the bottom could fall out of her world. As many times as it had, she felt as if she'd spent years holding her breath, waiting for it to happen all over again.

She felt that way now, as if she were holding her breath. She'd worked hard to ignore the old feelings of helplessness and insecurity the talk resurrected. But because of Ed Travers's son those feelings were there once more, hovering beneath the surface, threatening to rise up at any moment and resurrect the memories she had worked so hard to bury.

She *wasn't* helpless. It had taken a while, but she'd learned to manage well enough on her own. She was content with what she had. And heaven knew she was busy enough. The sense-of-security part was more of a work in progress, but in the past couple of years, she'd made headway there, too.

Or so she was telling herself as the low drone of a car engine filtered through the cold March air.

Emmy froze in her tracks. From where she had just emerged from the woods, she could see the BMW with New York plates slow as it approached the white, two-story house with its wide, welcoming front porch and the Wedgwood-blue trim she'd painted last summer.

Continuing past the house toward the stable she'd converted into a garage, the car crunched to a stop beneath the skeletal branches of a sycamore tree.

A low growl came from near her knee.

Only now noticing that Rudy had stopped chasing the squirrel he'd terrorized only moments ago and planted himself at her side, she touched the top of his big head.

"It's okay, boy," she murmured, reassured by his loyal presence. "We'll just see what he wants."

Across the blanket of white, she watched a tall, dark-haired man emerge from the car. The door closed with a crack that sounded like a gunshot a moment before she saw Jack Travers glance toward the house.

She had been barely twelve years old the last time she'd seen him. The fifteen years since then had erased many of the day-to-day memories of when he and his family had lived nearby, but she remembered well enough how she'd felt about him. He'd been like a big brother to her—or how she had imagined a big brother would be, since she'd never had any siblings. At least, that was the way she'd thought of him until he'd become just like his father and turned on his friends, too.

She had never seen him lose his temper as she'd heard he'd done. Certainly not with her. But it had been Jack who had first taught her that a person really couldn't count on anyone but family. Since she had no family left, she pretty much didn't count on anyone but herself anymore.

With his hands on the hips of his jeans, his heavy jacket open and making his shoulders look impossibly wide, he looked from the house to the plume of smoke and steam rising from the distant sugar house. As he did, he finally noticed her standing there.

Her stomach tightened as he started toward her. She remembered him being big. As he moved closer, his breath trailing off in the brisk air, he seemed even taller than she remembered, his build more athletic, more…powerful.

She hadn't heard what he did for a living. She wasn't sure anyone even knew. But he had an intensity about him as he approached, an air of success and command that seemed unmistakable. She'd seen the type before. Men like him, along with their equally intense, successful and demanding wives or girlfriends had been guests of the B and B she and her mom had converted their home into after her father died.

She saw his eyes narrow on her as he drew closer, his focus never leaving her face. Trying not to look as wary as she felt, she openly studied him back. A striking maturity carved the lean, almost elegant features that were more familiar than she'd thought they would be.

His mother had once been her mother's good friend. As he stopped in front of her, she could see a strong resemblance to Ruth Travers in the gleaming black of his short, neatly trimmed hair, his coal-dark lashes. Yet, there was nothing remotely feminine about the man. Certainly not the broad, intelligent brow, the piercing blue of his eyes or the carved lines of his mouth as it curved in a cautious smile.

She didn't remember him being so blatantly handsome. But then, she'd been a young girl when he'd left and, being a late bloomer, handsome to her had been her horse.

As his assessing glance slowly moved from the fleece cap covering her head down her slender frame and back to her unadorned face, he seemed to recognize her, too.

"Hi, Emmy." The deep tones of his rich, rumbling voice sounded as guarded as his expression. "It's been a long time. I'm Jack. Travers," he added, since she'd given no indication at all that he was familiar to her.

"I know who you are."

He had a small cleft in his chin. She noticed it when he gave her a grim little nod of acknowledgment. "Yeah," he murmured. "I suppose you do." A muscle in his jaw twitched as his glance slid from her toward the smoke and steam rising above the trees from the sugar house. "Is your father around?"

"My dad?" The question wasn't one she'd expected. "My dad died a long time ago."

He opened his mouth. Closing it again, the dark slashes of his eyebrows jammed together like lightning bolts.

"Ed died?" Incredulity marked his tone. "I mean, I'm

sorry," he hurried to amend, clearly caught off-guard by the news. "I had no idea." He shook his head, openly searching her face. "When?"

"Twelve years ago."

That seemed to throw him, too.

"What about your mom?" he ventured when she offered nothing else. "Can I talk to her?"

Emmy took a step back. It was as apparent as the latent tension radiating from his big body that he had no idea of the events that had eventually destroyed both of her parents, and robbed her youth of nearly every trace of security.

That blissful ignorance almost felt like an insult, and that insult felt strangely painful. "My mother is gone, too."

At her quiet reply, Jack felt a strange, sinking sensation in his chest. He knew how close she had been to her mom. She had absolutely worshiped her father.

"Emmy," he said, scrambling for words as he searched the delicate lines of her face. "I'm sorry about your parents. I really am. I didn't know about either of them," he admitted, hating how pitifully inadequate the words and the explanation sounded. "Neither did Mom. She'll be sorry to hear about them, too."

He watched her glance shy from his as she took another step back.

An uncomfortable moment later, she murmured, "Thank you."

Jack had forgotten how succinct some New Englanders could be with their responses. But he had the feeling Emmy wasn't simply being concise. Her brevity and the way she edged from him made it abundantly clear that she had no use for either him or his presence.

He wasn't surprised at all by how distrustful she seemed of him. What he hadn't been prepared for, however, was how much the quiet vulnerability he'd remembered about her touched him now.

He remembered her as a small and quiet child, all skinny arms, legs and long dark red hair. She'd trailed after him like a puppy, constantly asking questions, giggling when he teased her. She had reminded him of his little sister, Liz. And, he supposed, when she'd been around, he'd watched out for her much as he had his little sister, too.

Until the day he'd so clearly let her down.

He had never forgotten the last time he'd seen her, or the haunted look in her luminous gray eyes. He'd come that day to return the spare keys for her dad's truck, the one he had used in the sugar bush to haul dead snags for him. Emmy had stood on the porch beside her distraught father, holding his hand. As he'd given her dad the keys, he'd looked down to see Emmy looking up at him, her eyes huge as she silently begged him to do something to change everything back to the way it had been.

He didn't remember what was said between him and Stan, if anything at all. All he remembered were the silent tears of incomprehension that had rolled down Emmy's cheeks in the moments before he'd turned away.

He had never forgotten that look—the sadness, the bewilderment.

"I suppose you're who I need to talk to, then," he said, swearing that look was still there. So was the quietness about her. Only, now she seemed far more reserved than timid. And she was definitely no longer a little girl.

Her unadorned mouth was lush, the color of ripe peaches

against skin that look so clear and soft it practically invited a man to touch. He couldn't tell much about her slender shape beneath her heavy parka. But with her delicate features framed by the cap covering her hair, she looked as ethereal as a Botticelli angel and as fragile as glass.

"Can we go inside?" he asked, mentally regrouping to change his approach. "I only need a few minutes."

As if even a few more seconds was too much to ask, she immediately turned away. "I'm sorry. I don't have time to visit."

His hand shot out. Grabbing her arm, he stepped in front of her, blocking her retreat. There were things he had to say. He couldn't let her go until he did. He just couldn't remember what those things were as her cautious glance jerked to his and wariness hovered around her like a mist. Even through her jacket's thick layer of down, he swore he felt her muscles stiffen.

With the fog of their breath mingling between them, he was close enough to see the slivers of silver and pewter in her beautiful eyes. Close enough to see the tiny creases in the fullness of her lower lip. Her skin might invite a man to touch, but her mouth fairly begged to be kissed.

The tightening low in his gut made him go still.

So did her dog's low, feral growl.

Suddenly as aware of the canine's teeth as he was the woman warily watching him, he let her go. He'd braced himself for a less-than-welcoming reception, but things weren't going at all as he'd expected.

"I didn't come just to visit, Emmy." With another glance toward the fifty pounds of fur and snarl that had yet to move from her side, he took a step back himself. "There's something I need to do, but I can't if you won't hear me out."

"If you're here to tell me you bought the property next door, it's not necessary. Everyone already knows."

He would have been surprised if everyone hadn't. "I take it the local grapevine is still intact."

"Word gets around."

"Word in this case is incomplete. No one knows what I want to do with that land."

"What you do with it is your business." Deliberately she moved around him. "And the community council's. They'll try to block whatever you do."

"The community council has nothing to say about this," he insisted, stepping into her path again, mindful of her guard dog. "I bought it to give it back to your parents."

Blocked in her tracks once more, she glanced back up. An uncertain frown shadowed the gray of her eyes.

"My father passed away last year," he explained before she could decide to bolt again. "Mom never felt right about what had happened between our families. Neither did I. I want to give the property back. And to apologize.

"I hadn't realized your parents were gone," he told her, relieved that she was staying put. He wondered what had happened to Stan and Cara, decided now wasn't the time to ask. "When I checked with the real estate broker I used to see if the property was available, I was told that Larkin Maple Products was still in operation. I assumed your dad was still running it, so the quitclaim deed I brought is in his name."

He touched the jacket pocket that held that deed, thinking of what he needed to do now. "I'll redraw it for you. It won't take long. I just need to know your full name. I've always known you only as Emmy."

His glance shot to her left hand. The way she had her cuff pulled to her palm, he couldn't tell if she was wearing a ring. "Is it still Larkin, or are you married now?"

For a moment all Emmy could do was stare at the man blocking her path to the sugar house.

He wanted to give back the property. Of all the possible scenarios she might have imagined, this one had never occurred to her. It had apparently never occurred to anyone.

Her only thought now was that he'd made a long trip for nothing.

"My name doesn't matter."

"Of course it does. I can't change the deed without it."

"You don't need to change it."

"Emmy," he said, suddenly sounding terribly patient. "I'm not a tax attorney and I'm not sure what estate laws are here, but it's to your advantage to have the deed recorded in your name. That way there will be no questions. No hassles. It'll just be yours."

"I don't want it."

The dark slashes of his eyebrows merged. It seemed he wasn't prepared for that, either.

They were even, she supposed. She wasn't at all prepared herself. Not for his unexpected offer. And definitely not for his disquieting presence. As he towered over her, his cool blue eyes intent on her face, she could practically feel his tension snake inside her. The sensation disturbed her as much as the odd heat his scrutiny caused to radiate from her breasts to her belly.

Pulling her glance from his, she let it fall to where the

hem of his comfortably worn jeans bunched over a pair of heavy and expensive hiking boots. She didn't feel terribly trusting of him, and he unnerved her in ways she wasn't prepared to consider, but it wasn't like her to be unfair.

His father was responsible for what had happened to her family. And Jack had earned a reputation, too. Everyone knew he was responsible for the scar that hooked down from the corner of Joe Sheldon's mouth. Still, he had come to apologize. For himself, apparently. And for his mother. It sounded as if the matter had weighed for a long time on Ruth Travers.

As badly as Emmy wanted the past to stay there, she couldn't deny someone their need to try to set it right.

"I accept your apology," she told him. She had no desire, however, to hear whatever else he might have said beyond *I'm sorry*. All she wanted was for him to leave. "But I have no need of anything else.

"Please excuse me." Ducking her head again, she backed away, hoping he would just let her go. She'd lost her appetite for supper. Even if she hadn't, she had no time to put anything together now. "I'm boiling," she said, using the sugar-makers' term for making syrup. "I have to get back to work."

Wanting desperately to avoid the feelings and memories his presence elicited, she quickly retraced her path toward the sugar house, Rudy on her heels. Part of her couldn't believe how discourteous she was being. No one ever came to her home that she didn't take a minute to visit with them. But, then, her callers were inevitably neighbors or summer guests of her bed-and-breakfast, and she would invite them in to talk while she worked. More often than not she offered coffee or cocoa to go with their conversation. Or, in summer, when she worked in her garden, she offered lemonade or iced tea she made by setting a clear jug of water and tea bags in the sun because the tea tasted sweeter that way.

The twinge of guilt she felt leaving him standing there faded beneath an equally inherent need for self-preservation. It was probably horribly selfish of her, she admitted, watching Rudy race ahead, but she was far more interested in preserving the already shaken tranquillity she'd finally found than in being hospitable.

Emmy wasn't running, but she wasn't wasting any time getting away from him, either.

With that less-than-encouraging thought, Jack jammed his hands on his hips and watched Emmy motion her loping dog toward the trees and the distant sugar house.

It wasn't often that he underestimated a situation. As driven and determined as he could be when it came to achieving an end, he'd learned to plan for contingencies, to expect the unexpected and always have a plan B. With everything else he'd been dealing with lately, however, he'd obviously forgotten to consider that it could be a Larkin other than Stan running the sugaring business.

Once he'd learned that the operation still existed, he had simply assumed Stan was still running it. He had considered that Stan and Cara could be divorced by now, but it had never occurred to him that the man would have passed away, much less that his wife would have, too.

He definitely hadn't considered that the property would be refused.

The cold breeze carried off the fog of his frustrated

breath. For the past month he'd felt as if he'd been running a marathon. Now he felt as if he'd just run himself straight into a wall. Not that a wall would stop him. He just needed to find a way over, under or around the obstruction. Given that this particular obstruction wouldn't even talk to him at the moment, he headed back to his car.

It had been his goal to acquire and return the property ever since he and his mother had found a copy of the papers securing the money Stan had borrowed from him in his dad's desk. They had gone through the desk the day after his father died looking for insurance papers and, for the first time in years, he and his mom had talked about what had happened in Maple Mountain.

From the time his father had moved them all to Maine to escape the ostracism that had befallen the entire family, the subject had been forbidden in their home. That meant no one could talk about the way the locals had condemned his father for foreclosing on Stan's property. Or how his mother's friends had backed away from her because guilt by association condemned her, too. She'd told him she hadn't been able to tell anyone how opposed she'd been to what his father had done because he was her husband, and it hadn't felt right to speak publicly against him.

Jack understood all too well the dilemma his mother had faced. He'd often hoped he'd misunderstood what had happened, and that there had been some greater justification for his father betraying his friendship with Stan the way he had. He'd hoped his clashes with his former friends when they'd called his father a thief and backstabber had been justified, too. At the time, he had refused to stand back and not defend his family name—though looking back now, he figured the anger he'd felt had less to do with the pushing and shoving that had come with the taunting than the fact that he'd felt so betrayed himself.

At seventeen, he had been torn between loyalty to a father he'd looked up to and feeling that what his father had done was totally wrong. But the day they'd found the papers, his mother had confirmed that he hadn't misunderstood the basic facts at all. Stan Larkin had only borrowed five thousand dollars on property worth three times that. Granted, Stan hadn't paid the loan when it was due, but his father hadn't been willing to give him extra time and had sold the property for a fraction of what it had been worth. His dad's only concern had been getting the money back without any further delay.

His mom had since shared a few details that had apparently justified the action in his father's mind. And, taken literally, Jack could see the man's logic. His father had worked hard for his money, and he'd been watching out for his own family. But in Jack's mind that didn't forgive why he hadn't sold the property for nearer to what it was worth and given Stan the difference.

All his father had cared about was getting back his own. And he had. But it had cost him and his family dearly.

Jack passed an upright post supporting a wood oval carved with *Larkin's Maple Products* and turned on to the snow-packed and winding mountain road that led the two miles into the little community. As he did, he had the disturbing feeling that what his father had done might have cost the Larkins even more.

That uncomfortable thought curled like a fist in Jack's gut.

There wasn't much room for deviation in his schedule,

but he wouldn't leave without setting things as straight as he could. He'd planned to be home no later than midnight that night. But as long as he could be back in Manhattan by five tomorrow afternoon, he would have time to finish packing up his apartment before the movers arrived Monday morning. As soon as they left, he would head for the office he was taking over in Boston.

From the day he'd started, nine years ago, he'd systematically worked his way up the corporate ladder of the billion-dollar Atlantic Commercial Development Corporation. He'd put in practically twenty-four hours, seven days a week for the past two years for his latest promotion to regional vice president. His perks alone were worth three times his original salary. Because he wasn't through climbing yet, and because he had major projects on the table, he didn't want anything to interfere with his 7:00 a.m. breakfast meeting Tuesday morning with his staff.

In the meantime he needed Emmy's legal name. He also needed a notary public to notarize his signature, and a photocopier to copy the new document. He had a blank quitclaim deed in the file in his back seat that he'd brought in case Stan had wanted his wife's or their company's name on the document, so redrawing it wouldn't be a problem. Once that was done, he'd head back to the Larkin place and hope Emmy would be more receptive to accepting the property. Heaven knew he didn't want it.

Chapter Two

Maple Mountain would never be known as a destination spot. As far as Jack was concerned, the place was lucky simply to have a spot on the map. Except for the three seasonal festivals the community sponsored to raise money for its coffers, most visitors were simply passing through.

Those who did stop for a night could find accommodation at one of the few bed-and-breakfasts in the area, though they were seldom open in winter except for Maple Sugar Days, or they could stay at the Maple Mountain Motor Inn—which stayed open mostly to accommodate the guy who ran the snow plow when the weather turned.

With no other option, Jack checked into the motor inn. The long, low building on the narrow main road consisted of eight rooms that opened on to a snow-covered parking lot and a postage-stamp-size reception area decorated with knotty pine walls and an impressive set of antlers. The sign on the front door claimed the place to have the friendliest accommodations in Vermont's Northern Kingdom.

He didn't know about the accommodations themselves, but their owners didn't exactly live up to the advertising. The Mrs. part of the operation didn't, anyway. The late-thirty-something Hanna Talbot, whose grandparents had owned the motel before they'd retired years ago, had taken one look at him when she'd answered the desk bell and her smile had died.

"What can I do for you, Jack?" she asked, sounding as if she'd heard he was around.

"I need a room for the night. Do you have anything available?"

He'd asked for the sake of polite conversation. All eight room keys hung on their hooks. The parking lot was empty. Yet, for a few rather uncomfortable seconds, he thought the woman might actually claim they were booked.

"I'll need your driver's license," she said instead.

He reached for his wallet, only feeling slightly relieved. He didn't remember much about the curly-haired brunette other than that she was a few years older than he was and that her family had always owned the place. She clearly remembered him, though. Or, at least, judging from the chill that was definitely more censure than natural reserve, she remembered his family.

Cooking smells, the low drone of a television and children's voices drifted in from the open door behind her.

"New York," she said, writing down his address. "I thought your family moved to Maine."

"They did." He handed over a credit card, wondering at

the length of some people's memories. "I'm the only one in New York."

Looking as if she couldn't imagine why he would have wanted to come back, she pushed his license across the shiny wood surface. "Long drive."

It had been a long drive, he thought. A little over six hours, actually. Three of those on snow-packed roads. But driving made more sense than flying or taking the train. There were no direct flights from JFK or LaGuardia to the nearest airport in Montpelier, so it took as much time to drive as it did to fly. At least behind the wheel of his car, he felt as if he were constantly making progress.

There wasn't much that frustrated him more than hanging around airports accomplishing nothing. Except, possibly, accomplishing nothing while being stuck overnight in a place he didn't want to be.

Feeling that the less he said the better, Jack's only response was a faint, acknowledging smile as the woman handed his card back.

The proprietress of the little mom-and-pop motel didn't seem to expect a comment, anyway.

"There's a potluck at the community center tonight, so Dora's is closed," she informed him, speaking of the diner down the road. "My family's headin' over there now. Since there's nowhere else to get a meal, I suppose I can bring you somethin' for supper from there."

She seemed to know that he wouldn't want to eat at a community dinner himself. Or maybe she was thinking more that he wouldn't be welcome there. From Emmy's flat tone when she'd said everyone knew he'd bought the acreage next to hers, he'd be willing to bet everyone at that dinner would have an opinion about that acquisition, too. No Travers had been able to do anything right by the time they'd moved. He was getting the distinct feeling from this woman that no Travers could do anything right now, either.

What bothered him even more was the surprising depth of her apparent disapproval of him. He'd barely known the woman. Yet, her censure felt as fresh as what he'd felt from others when his family had left.

"I appreciate the offer, but I'll get something on my own." The burger he'd grabbed at a drive-through five hours ago had long since worn off, but he wasn't about to put her out. "What about the burger place?" A little repetition wouldn't kill him. "Is it still here?"

"Closed for the winter. Most everything around here is."

Hunger seemed to increase in direction proportion to his diminishing culinary options. "How about the general store?" He'd seen the lights on inside when he'd driven past it a few minutes ago. "How late is it open?"

A child's voice grew louder. Another matched it, insisting on the return of the video game controls. After aiming a weary glance toward the doorway, she shifted it to the old-fashioned cuckoo clock near the antlers. "'Bout another five minutes."

"One last thing." Not wanting to keep her any longer, he picked up the room key she'd set on the counter, stuffed it into his coat pocket. "Do you know Emmy Larkin?"

Quick curiosity narrowed the woman's eyes. "Of course I do."

"You wouldn't happen to know her full name, would you?"

With a Travers asking after a Larkin, curiosity turned to distrust.

"Why would you want to know that?"

"There's something I need to take her."

"Then, I suppose you can ask her yourself when you see her."

Faced with that protective and practical New England logic, Jack picked up his receipt, slid it into his pocket. With a resigned nod, he lifted his hand as he backed toward the door. He wouldn't be getting any information here. "I suppose I can. Thanks for the room."

"She'll be sugarin', so I wouldn't think she'd have time for you tonight."

"I'm not going until morning."

"She won't be there then. Tomorrow's Sunday. Services don't get out until eleven."

He couldn't tell if the woman was trying to discourage him or be helpful. "Thanks," he said again, leaning heavily toward the former.

"Checkout's at noon."

"Got it," he replied, and escaped into the cold before he had to deal with any more of her "friendliness."

The gray of dusk was rapidly giving way to the darkness of night. There were no streetlights in Maple Mountain to illuminate the narrow two-lane road that served as its only thoroughfare. Rather unoriginally called Main, the road curved on its way through the sleepy little community, a ribbon of white lined by four-foot banks of snow left behind by a plow.

It was barely six o'clock on a Saturday night, yet the dozen businesses and buildings that comprised the core of the community were closed and as dark as the hills above them. The only lights came from the general store down near the curve of the road and the headlamps of two cars that turned onto the short street that ended at the white clapboard community center.

Hunching his shoulders against the evening's deepening chill, he crossed the packed snow of the motel's parking lot and headed to the store. He could grab something there to take back to his room for dinner and breakfast. With any luck, he could also get Emmy's full name. He would have asked at the post office, had it not been closed.

When he finally stepped inside the store, he could see that the place had hardly changed. It smelled as it always had, faintly of must and burning wood from the potbellied stove in the middle of the room. A wooden pickle barrel topped by a checkerboard sat a comfortable distance from that radiating warmth.

The dairy cooler still occupied the back wall. Rows of groceries filled the four short aisles to his left. The walls themselves still held the same eclectic mix of sundries. Snowshoes competed for space with frying pans. Sparkplugs were stacked above empty gas cans and saw blades.

The only staple missing from his memories of the place were the old men who'd routinely congregated around the game board to discuss local politics, play checkers and lie to each other about the size of the fish they caught in their fishing shacks on the frozen lake. Either they'd all died or they'd gone home to supper.

The short, squat owner hadn't changed much, either. Agnes Waters's short brown curls were now half-silver, and the laugh lines around her eyes looked deeper than they'd been when he'd played high school sports with her youngest son. But her hazel eyes looked as sharp as ever and, even now, her memory rivaled an elephant's. Seeing who her customer was her expression registered clear disapproval.

Jack could practically feel his back rise at the suspicious way she looked him over. He hadn't counted on the defensiveness he would feel in this place. But then, he'd been so focused on his promotion, moving and acquiring the property to give back to the Larkins that he hadn't thought about how resentful of other's attitudes he'd become by the time his family had left there.

The feeling, however, had wasted no time coming back. "Mrs. Waters," he said, forcing an intentionally civil nod.

Geese in flight were silk-screened across the front of her heavy green sweatshirt. Obliterating half the flock as she crossed her arms, she gave him a tight little nod. "Hello, Jack. Been a while."

His tone remained even. "A while," he agreed, refusing to let old resentments get the better of him. "I just need to pick up a few things," he explained. "I know you're getting ready to close, so I'll hurry."

"I saw you come through town earlier," she told him, stopping him in his tracks. Ignoring any need she had to close up and go home, she checked him over from haircut to hiking boots. "You seem to have done well for yourself." Her sharp eyes narrowed. "What is it you do?"

"Do?"

"For a living."

"Commercial development." By noon tomorrow everyone in the community would know what he drove and what

he did to earn his keep. He'd bet his new corner office on
it. "Why?"

"I was afraid it was something like that," she claimed,
managing to look displeased and vindicated at the same time.

"Excuse me?"

"Your occupation." Looking as if she couldn't imagine
what he didn't understand, she tightened her hold on the
geese. "I had the feelin' you were going to develop that
land the minute I heard you'd bought it. I can tell you right
now that you can forget about whatever it is you're plan-
nin' to put on that parcel, Jack Travers. We don't want
commercial development here. The community council
won't stand for it. I know. I'm on it."

His voice went flat. "I'm not building anything," he assured her, and hitched his thumb toward the back wall. "I'm
just going to grab what I need and get out of here. Okay?"

Pure confusion pleated the woman's forehead as he
turned toward a display of chips, grabbed a bag and headed
for the back wall.

The woman was getting herself all worked up for nothing. The old bat had taken a fragment of information,
thrown in a lot of supposition and dug in her heels to op-
pose him without a clue about what was actually going on.
Unfortunately, while telling her to can the attitude would
have made him feel better, it wouldn't do a thing to help
him get the information he needed.

Wanting only to get that information and get out of
there, he headed back with his hastily chosen purchases
and started setting them on the counter.

"Do you know where I can find a notary and a copier
around here?"

"The library has a copy machine." Ignoring his other request along with his packages, the pleats in her forehead deepened. "If you're not building anything, why did you buy the old Larkin parcel?"

"It's not for business," he assured her again. He pushed a toothbrush and a disposable razor toward her. He couldn't find shaving cream. He'd just have to use soap for his shave in the morning. "It's personal."

"Then you're not putting up condos?"

"I'm not putting up anything," he repeated, adding a package of Danish, lunch meat and a cola. Had he been home, he'd be at the little Italian place around the corner from his apartment, ordering penne with mushrooms and a glass of good wine. "The library," he repeated, thinking the wine sounded especially good. With Agnes frowning at him, so did a shot of anything with a burn to it. "Thanks. What about Emmy Larkin's full name? Do you know what it is?"

The woman had yet to ring up a single item. "What are you up to with Emmy?"

He bit back a sigh. "I'm not up to anything."

"Well, you'd better not cause her any trouble. That girl's been through enough without whatever it is you're up to out there making her life any harder than it needs to be. She's lost…"

"She told me about her parents," he cut in, saving her the trouble of mentioning their deaths since it seemed she was about to. "I'm sorry to hear they're gone."

He wasn't sure why, but for an oddly uncomfortable moment, he thought the older woman might say that he certainly should be, as if he, or at least one of his kin, was somehow responsible for those particular losses. It was that kind of accusation tightening her expression.

The disturbing feeling he'd had when he'd left the Larkin place—the feeling that they had lost more than just land and profits because of what his dad had done—compounded itself as Agnes finally punched in the price of the chips.

"How is she doing?" he asked, not knowing what to make of the new edge to the reproach he'd experienced all those years ago. The same censure he'd picked up from Hanna Talbot was definitely there. But with Agnes it felt almost as if his father's transgression, along with his own, perhaps, had been more...recent.

Edging the Danish toward her, he tried to shake the odd feeling. It had been fifteen years. There was nothing "recent" about it.

"Is she able to handle the sugaring operation okay?"

"She does as well as any of the other sugar makers," the older woman admitted, punching in the cost of the small package. "Her B and B is one of the nicest around, too. Works hard, that girl."

Apparently deciding she wasn't getting anything else out of him, she punched in the razor, too.

He handed over the package of sliced turkey. "She runs a bed-and-breakfast?"

"Summer and fall. She turned down a scholarship to study architecture and design when her mom took ill so she could stay and help Cara run the place. She did most of the redecorating herself."

The cash-register drawer popped open when she rang up the last of the items and hit the total key. Over the heavy footfall on the porch that announced another customer's approach, she said, "That'll be $10.80."

The unexpected information about Emmy had Jack wondering what else he could learn from the woman as he reached for his billfold. Thinking he might hang around for a minute after her customer left, he glanced toward the door. It opened with the ring of the bell, a rush of icy air and the voice of a man apologizing even before he was all the way inside.

"I know you're getting ready to close, Agnes. But I told Amber I'd pick up baking soda on my way home and just now remembered. She'll have my hide if I come home without it."

A man wearing a deputy's heavy, brown leather jacket and serge uniform pants pulled off his fur-lined hat as he shoved the door closed. Looking prepared to offer a neighborly greeting to whoever was at the counter, he stood with a broad smile on his rugged face for the two seconds it took recognition to hit.

The burly ex-high-school line-backer swore. Or maybe, Jack thought, the terse oath he heard had been inside his own head.

It seemed like some perverse quirk of fate that Joe Sheldon should now be a sheriff's deputy. One of the last times they'd seen each other, the old deputy Joe had apparently replaced had almost arrested Jack for nearly breaking Joe's jaw.

Lifting his hand, Joe touched the short silvery scar that curved from the left corner of his mouth. It appeared that he hadn't forgotten the encounter, either.

The guy's voice sounded like gravel rolling in a can. "I heard you were back, Larkin."

"He said he's not developing that property." Agnes offered the pronouncement as she bagged Jack's purchases. "But he's asking after Emmy."

Joe took a measured step toward him, his rough-hewn features set, his eyes assessing. He looked beefier than he had as a cocky teenager, solid in a way that told Jack he wouldn't want to tangle with him now. Not that he wouldn't be able to hold his own if he had to. He usually started his mornings with a five-mile run and pumped iron at the gym four days a week for no other reason than to keep his head clear. He'd always been a physical man, always felt best using the pent-up energy in his muscles. But he'd fought all those years ago only because he had felt forced to defend his family's name. The battles he took on now were won by sheer determination, ambition and drive.

Joe's eyes narrowed. "What do you want with her?"

Jack wanted no hassles. He also had no intention of answering to anyone but a Larkin. "That's between Emmy and me."

"Not if you cause her or anyone else around here any trouble." His one-time teammate's voice lowered with warning. "You do and you answer to me."

Pushing bills across the counter, Jack picked up his bag, paper crackling. He had no intention of feeding an old grudge. His or Joe's. "I didn't come here to cause trouble," he informed him, wondering what it was they thought he was going to do to the woman. Or anyone else, for that matter. "Not for her. Not for anyone."

"Then, why are you here?"

"To set things right." Steel edged his tone. That same

unbending resolve glinted in his eyes as he walked past the man he could have sworn was trying to stare him down.

"How do you intend to do that?" Joe demanded over the tinkle of the bell as Jack pulled open the door.

"That's between me and Emmy, too," he called back, and closed the door a little harder than he probably should have.

He hadn't forgotten how narrow and protective the small-town mentality could be. In Maple Mountain the sins of the father carried right down to his offspring. The fact that the offspring had defended the father was obviously remembered, as well. He just hadn't thought he'd have to deal with anyone other than the Larkins.

The muscles in his jaw working, he headed through the dark and cold to his less-than-welcoming motel room. The good news when he got there was that he didn't have to deal with anyone else—and that the only homage to the local wildlife on his room's knotty pine walls was a painting of a moose. The bad news was that he still didn't know Emmy's full name.

That didn't do much for his mood, either.

Emmy knew Jack hadn't left Maple Mountain. Agnes had called last evening while she'd been filling tins with syrup, a task that couldn't easily be interrupted, and left the news flash on her answering machine.

She hadn't called Agnes back. Nor had she done anything other than thank her for her call after services that morning before excusing herself when the elderly minister's wife, bless her, rescued her from the speculation Agnes had clearly been itching to share.

It had been Emmy's experience that the less she let on

that something was a problem, the less others treated it like one. She'd also learned that life was less complicated when the personal parts of it weren't served up for public consumption. She tried hard not to look back, to focus her energies on the present, and allowed herself to look no farther ahead than the next season.

The only season on her mind at the moment was the current one. As she bounced her rugged and reliable old pickup truck over a berm of snow at the edge of her driveway, her only thoughts were of getting home and to her chores before she lost any more of the day. It was already one o'clock in the afternoon.

The pastor's wife had asked a favor of her, and completely sidetracked her from her original plan to be home before noon.

Sidetracking her now was the black sedan parked by the old sycamore—and the sight of Jack standing outside the stable that now served as a garage.

He hadn't struck her as the sort who would give up easily. Knowing he'd stayed last night, she'd pretty much expected him to come back, too. She'd just rather hoped that he would come back, find her gone and leave.

Not sure if she felt threatened by his persistence or relieved by it, she drove past him and through the open doors of the utilitarian white building.

What he had come back to do had been on her mind all evening. It had been the first thing on her mind that morning. Part of her, the part that felt unkind and uncomfortable about how she'd walked away from him yesterday, had actually considered stopping by the motel to apologize for being so insensitive. She felt awful for the way she'd treated him. After she'd had a chance to truly consider what it must have taken for him to come back, and after she'd acknowledged the courage, the integrity, and the basic sense of decency he would have to possess to even want to make amends after so long, she'd felt even worse.

She hadn't even thanked him for his apology.

Another part of her, the more protective part, had hoped he would tire of waiting for her and be halfway to the free-way—which was probably, she figured, why she really hadn't minded the delay getting home.

Feeling no less torn by his presence now, she climbed out of her truck and squeezed past the cherry-red snowmobile she used to haul skids of firewood from the woodshed to the sugar house, or to get into town when the snow was too deep to drive there. The sun that had shone so brightly yesterday had given way to a ceiling of pale gray. From that solid layer of clouds, a few tiny snowflakes drifted down as she headed into the open expanse between the outbuilding and her house.

They weren't supposed to get snow until that evening, she thought, looking from the sky to the tall and totally disconcerting man closing the distance between them. He wore the same clothes he'd worn yesterday, the dark-gray jacket that made his shoulders look so wide, the darker-gray turtleneck and sweater, the worn jeans that molded his lean hips and long, powerful legs. He'd shaved, though. She could tell from the smoothness of the skin on his strong, too-attractive face, and the nick under his chin.

That tiny vulnerability made her feel guilty for his long wait. He'd shaved before he'd come to see her.

"Come to the sugar house," she said, saving him the

trouble of telling her he needed to talk to her. "I need to get the fire stoked and bring in more wood. We can talk there."

A fleece cap in the same shade of pale pink as her turtleneck poked from the side pocket of her quilted black coat. Without the cap she'd worn yesterday, the spitting snowflakes clung to the top of her head, caught in her high, swinging ponytail. Watching her walk away, it seemed to Jack that her shining baby-fine hair seemed darker, more auburn than the deep red he remembered. Richer. Softer.

He'd heard somewhere that natural redheads tended to be rather volatile. He'd never dated one to know how much truth there was to the claim, though one particular blonde had proved explosive enough. Emmy, however, didn't strike him at all as a woman prone to fits of temper. The sense of quiet control about her gave him the feeling she'd go as far out of her way as necessary to avoid confrontation.

Watching her ponytail bounce, he started after her. She also possessed an absolute gift for throwing curves. Rather than meeting the wall of resistance he'd expected, she hadn't seemed all that opposed to finding him waiting.

Telling himself to be grateful, he glanced back toward her truck. Heavy tire chains wrapped the tires. Bags of sand lay in the bed for better traction. It was the vehicle itself that had first caught his attention, though. The old workhorse of a pickup looked very much like the one her father had driven fifteen years ago.

"Was everything all right this morning?" he asked, thinking the truck had to be pushing thirty years old by now.

"Everything's fine. Why?"

"I just thought that with the sap running, you'd be in a hurry to get back and start boiling."

Instead of heading for the sugar house, she'd angled toward her home.

"The minister's wife asked me to do a feasibility study for the restoration of the church. We started looking around," she said, snow crunching under their boots, "and I lost track of the time."

She truly had. For a while. There wasn't much that appealed to her more than the prospect of taking something old and falling apart and returning it to what it once had been. Just studying the 120-year-old building and researching its repair excited her. Or would have had she not been so aware of the man who'd just walked up beside her.

She could practically feel his frown on the side of her face.

"I thought you turned down the scholarship."

She stopped in the snow, looking up at him as a tiny flake settled on her cheek. One clung to a strand of the dark hair falling over his wide forehead. Another drifted between them. "How do you know about that?"

"Agnes said you were going to study architecture and design, but that you turned down your scholarship to stay and help your mom."

The corner of her mouth quirked, half in acknowledgment, half in something that looked almost as if she might have expected as much.

"I did turn it down," she replied, but offered nothing else as she continued on.

"Then where did you learn what you'd need to know to restore a church?" he called after her.

"The same places I learned the plastering methods for the

walls and moldings when we restored the library. I ordered books and did research on the Internet. That led me to a restorer in Montpelier, so I spent a week one spring working with her. She came out later to check what we'd done."

Leaving him staring at her back, she headed up the shoveled steps to the back door of her house to let out her dog, then pulled open the aluminum storm door. The moment she opened the wooden one behind it, her impatient pet leaped past her in an exuberant blur of pale-gold fur, then practically slid to a stop ten feet from the porch when he noticed Jack standing a few yards away.

"It's okay, Rudy," she called, closing the doors to descend the stairs herself. "He's coming with us."

The animal instantly went from eyeing him to ignoring him. Looking like a mutt on a mission, he raced ahead to lift his leg on the side of a stump, then ran off, snow flying, to weave his way toward the distant gray building.

Clearly on a mission herself, Emmy hurried past Jack and along the packed path.

"The truck you were driving," he said, still thinking about it. "That isn't the same one I used to drive for your dad, is it?" It was the same make, but he'd thought that truck had been dark green, not dark blue.

He couldn't see her face, yet there was no mistaking her hesitation in the moments before she replied.

"No, it's not," she said, continuing on. "That one was wrecked."

"What happened?"

"It was in an accident. Rudy!" she called, putting a deliberate end to what he'd thought was harmless conversation. "This way, boy!"

She hurried ahead of him more quickly, glancing up as she entered the woods to cast a troubled glance through the bare tree branches.

Wondering what happened to the old truck, and even more curious about why she so obviously didn't want to talk about it, he looked up at that darkening gray ceiling. Tiny, sporadic flakes continued to fall.

When he'd checked the weather before he'd left yesterday, the report had been for sun through the weekend. Listening to the only radio station he'd been able to get in his car, since he'd needed something to do while he'd waited, the weatherman had mentioned a large front moving in that evening.

It looked to him as if that front were on its way in now.

Wanting to be gone before anything nasty developed, he lengthened his stride. He just had a few details he wanted cleared up before he left.

He still needed Emmy's full name so he could change the deed. There wouldn't be time today to get his signature notarized and make a copy of the document so he could leave the original with her, but he could get what he needed and mail it later. Having learned what he had about her, he also felt obligated to find out how she was managing the responsibilities she'd inherited. Then there was the niggling need to find out what had happened after his family had left. He couldn't seem to shake the feeling that the Travers were being held responsible for something more than he'd believed when he'd arrived.

First, though, he would let her talk. From the way she'd invited him to come with her, it was clear she had something she wanted to say.

Chapter Three

"Is that the wood you're taking in?" Emmy heard Jack ask as he pointed to the pallet of cordwood near the building's wide end door.

She told him it was, and that she'd take it in after she stoked the fire. She also needed to check the tanks on her gas generators in case the incoming weather took out the power, she reminded herself, opening the smaller door near the sugar house's only window. It was so much harder working in the sugar house with only oil lamps for light.

With the flip of the switch inside the door, the bright overhead bulbs illuminated the small but efficient space. The far end of the open room served as an office where she ran her invoices and made mailing labels with the computer. Nearer the door, stacked boxes of syrup waiting to be shipped and empty tins waiting to be filled obscured the rough wood wall behind the worktable where she packaged her finished product.

Aware of Jack walking in behind her, she moved past what took up the other end of the room; the four-by-twelve-foot-long stainless steel evaporating pan where she boiled down sap.

"Leave the door open for Rudy, would you?" she asked, grabbing a pair of battered leather gloves from the dwindling pile of wood beyond the pan.

Still wearing her good winter coat, she pulled the gloves on, opened the metal door of the fire arch built under the pan, and stoked the embers she'd banked last night. As she did, Jack stopped beside her with two quartered logs he'd picked up from the pile.

"Do you want me to bring in more wood while you do that?" he asked, holding the logs out to her.

Taking what he offered, she shoved them into the arch. "I'll do it in a minute."

"I don't mind carrying some in."

"That's not necessary. Really," she insisted, not wanting him to take the time. "I just need to get this going and fill the pan."

Sparks flew as raw wood hit glowing embers. Heat radiated toward her face. She felt heat at the back of her neck, too, where he stared down at it.

Disconcerted by the sensation, she shoved in two more logs and closed the door with a solid clang. Leaving her gloves on an upended log, and him standing where he was, she headed for the spigot at the opposite end of the long metal pan. An inch-wide main line carried the sap from the acres of tapped trees around and above the building to the storage tank. With a turn of a knob, she watched the watery liquid from the holding tank flow into the top of the pan, and took a deep breath.

With nothing else demanding her immediate attention, she prepared to do what she should have done yesterday, and felt totally ambivalent about doing now.

The weather-grayed building wasn't very large. Thirty feet by twenty, give or take a foot. She just hadn't realized how small that space could be until she turned to where Jack and his rather imposing presence seemed to dominate the entire room.

"I have to be honest with you," she quietly admitted, wanting to get her apology over with. "I'd hoped you would be gone when I got here. But I'm glad you came back. I didn't thank you for your apology yesterday," she explained, when his brow lowered at her admission. "After all this time, you could have easily just let the matter go.

"So thank you," she conceded, when she really wouldn't have minded at all if he'd been a man of lesser conscience. If he had considered everything over and done with all those years ago, she wouldn't just have been reminded of why she'd had to decline the scholarship she'd once desperately wanted to accept, or about the old truck he'd once driven, the one her dad had died in.

"I can only imagine how hard it was for you to come back here," she continued. "I just want you to know I appreciate the effort it must have taken. I appreciate your offer to return the land, too," she admitted, certain that acquiring it had also taken considerable effort and expense. "I can't accept it, but it was incredibly generous of you to offer it back.

"And your mom," she hurried on, compelled to offer him something in return. "Please tell her I especially appreciate knowing she hadn't felt right about what happened." It had never occurred to her that Ruth Travers would feel any particular remorse or regret about what had transpired. Locked in her twelve-year-old world at the time, and having grown up knowing only what she'd felt and what she'd heard from others, she had thought of all the Traverses the same way—as people who had hurt her and parents. "For my mom, one of the hardest parts of all that happened back then was losing her friendship."

Seconds ago Jack's only thought had been to ask why she wouldn't accept the property. His only thoughts now were of her quiet admission and of the mental image he could have sworn he'd erased.

"That was hard for my mom, too," he admitted. "I think she cried halfway to Maine." He had blocked the quiet sound of those tears and his father's hard silence with his headphones cranked nearly high enough to shatter his eardrums. "I don't know if anyone around here would believe it, but she really cared about your mom and the rest of her friends. She was pretty devastated by the way things turned out."

It had been hard on him and his little sister, too. On Liz, two years older than Emmy, because she'd also lost her friends. The girls at school hadn't throw accusations in her face as his peers had done, but they had excluded her, whispered behind her back, made her cry. He didn't mention that, though. From what he'd learned since yesterday, Emmy's life had fared far worse.

"Tell her I believe it." Sounding far more forgiving than

anyone else he'd encountered lately, she offered an equally pardoning smile. "What happened wasn't her doing."

"She'll be relieved that you know that."

He wanted that smile to be for him, too. He wanted to make sure she understood that it hadn't been his fault, either, that there wasn't anything he could have done to stop his father. But the moment was lost. The shadow of a smile she'd given him had already faded.

"I need to get the wood in," she said, and walked away.

Slipping off her coat, she hung it on a peg near the door, glancing back toward him as she did.

"Do you have a thermos in your car?"

"A thermos?"

"For coffee. Or cocoa." She nodded toward the coffee-maker at the far end of the long board that served as her desk. "I can make either and fill it for you."

He'd just been told he was leaving. He just wasn't sure how she'd managed it so graciously.

"Coffee," he said, because he was dying for a cup. There hadn't been anywhere other than the diner to buy any that morning, and he hadn't felt desperate enough for caffeine to encounter whoever had been in there. "But I don't have anything to put it in."

"I'll get you something." Apparently unwilling to let a minor detail slow down his departure, she reached for the quilted red-and-black flannel shirt hanging on another peg.

His frown landed squarely on her back. Without the bulk of a coat, it seemed to him that there wasn't much to her. At least not enough for what she apparently did around there. A sugaring operation was hard work. He knew. He'd worked with her father in the sugar bush thinning trees in the summer, running lines and tapping trees in the winter. He'd occasionally worked in this very room, hauling heavy buckets of hot syrup to the filter and stacking filled boxes of the finished product.

She needed to be sturdier. Heftier. She needed more muscle.

Not that there was anything wrong with her undeniably feminine shape, the purely male portion of his brain admitted. As his glance drifted over the seductive curve of her backside, then up to her raised arms, he felt the same unmistakable jolt of heat that had caught him so off guard yesterday. She'd tucked the soft-pink turtleneck she wore into the waist of slender dark-gray denims, revealing sweetly rounded breasts and a waist small enough he could almost span it with his hands.

The thought of having his hands anywhere on her sexy little body had him looking away even as she tugged on the heavy flannel shirt that practically swallowed her whole.

He was far better off thinking of her as the skinny little kid who'd barely been big enough at one time to stand at the long metal sink without a step stool. He remembered her dragging that stool around the room as she followed her dad, stepping up on it so she could watch him measure the sugar in the sap or the syrup, climbing down to lug a single piece of split wood for the fire.

An unfamiliar disquiet had him heading for the large door at the end of the room. Remembering her with the dad she'd adored, he could only imagine how hard it must have been for her to lose him. He knew how hard it had been to lose his own father, and they hadn't agreed on much of anything for years.

Not wanting to think about that, either, he pushed on the heavy door and jammed it open against the snowbank behind it. She couldn't object to his bringing the wood in now. He had to wait for his coffee.

Tiny snowflakes still drifted down as he gathered and carried in two large armloads. He was on his way in with a third when he turned to see her standing at the threshold holding a pair of large, worn leather gloves.

"You really don't need to do this," she said.

He walked past her, unloading his load on the growing stack. "You didn't need to make me coffee, either."

The coffee hadn't been an act of hospitality. It had been a hint. Apparently too courteous to point that out, she held out the gloves.

"Put them on. You don't need splinters."

He held his hand up, palm out. "Already got one," he said, but took the gloves anyway.

Giving him a look of resignation, or maybe it was forbearance, she pulled on her own gloves and silently went to work beside him.

Within minutes, the half cord of wood that had been outside was now inside, bits of bark and wood had been brushed from their clothes, and the big door was pulled closed.

"Thank you," she said, leaving him to toss his gloves next to where she'd just left hers on the replenished stack.

"No problem," he replied to her departing back and pulled at the Velcro tabs on his heavy jacket. Even with the side door still open and the inside air cool from the bigger door having been open, too, the small task had quickly warmed his muscles. From the fire inside it, the metal arch radiated heat like a large, squat furnace.

Vaguely aware of her dog barking somewhere in the distance, he looked from the crowded worktable to where she pulled a hair clip from her baggy shirt's pocket. "You don't do this all alone, do you?"

"Not all the time."

He was glad to hear that. Knowing she had help relieved him. A little.

"How much of the time?" he wanted to know, thinking Rudy's barking sounded more like excitement than warning.

As if she'd done it a thousand times before, she deftly whipped her ponytail into a knot and anchored it with the clip. "Charlie Moorehouse usually helps me."

He knew Charlie. Of him, anyway. He was one of the old guys who'd played checkers at the general store. "I thought Charlie had his own sugaring operation."

"He retired and sold it to the Hanleys a few years ago," she replied, speaking of another sugaring family in the area. "He gets cranky come sugaring time if he can't make syrup, so I asked him if he'd work for me."

Thinking it sounded as if she'd hired Charlie as much for the old guy's benefit as her own, he nodded toward the open door. "Is that who your dog's barking at?"

"Charlie won't be coming today. His gout has been acting up and his big toe is too painful to get a boot on."

Looking curious herself about who her dog seemed to be greeting, she was already moving to the doorway.

Curiosity promptly faded to caution when she stopped and looked back toward him.

"It's Joe," she said, and turned to check on the progress of the coffee.

Jack stifled a groan as he brushed back the sides of his jacket and jammed his hands on his hips. He'd figured he had another ten minutes to get the answers he sought before she started hinting again that he should leave. The absolute last thing he wanted right now was to be interrupted by a deputy with a chip the size of a tree on his shoulder.

"We still have a couple things to discuss, Emmy."

As if she knew exactly what he wanted, she sent a look of utter patience across the aged plank boards of the floor.

"I already told you, I appreciate what you offered, but I don't want it."

He opened his mouth, promptly closed it again. He wasn't going to argue with her now. Not with Joe on his way. There was one thing he thought she should know, however, in case the local deputy got any grandiose ideas about running him off.

"I'm not leaving until we've talked."

"We *have* talked."

"You talked," he countered. "You said what you had to say, but I never got started."

"Other than the property, there's nothing else to discuss."

"Actually there's a lot more. We haven't even started talking about you."

It was as clear as fresh sap that she had no idea why she should be a topic of discussion. It seemed equally apparent that she had no intention of indulging his interest, but she didn't have time to actually tell him that before Rudy ran through the door, tongue lolling, just ahead of the man who filled most of the doorway.

Wearing his uniform, his hat dangling from one hand, Joe absently leaned down to scratch the dog behind its ear.

As he performed the apparently routine gesture, he looked straight at Jack.

His bold brown eyes locked on eyes of piercing blue.

"Everything okay here, Emmy?" Joe asked.

The chill suddenly permeating the room had nothing to do with the cold outside. Emmy had never known the area's only law officer to be anything but easygoing. As far as she was concerned, Joe was a big, congenial teddy bear who spent more time checking in on folks to make sure nothing was amiss than doing actual law enforcement. But then she'd never seen him around anyone he held a grudge against. Or who obviously held one against him.

Her glance fixed on the scar at the corner of his mouth a moment before she turned it on the man pointedly holding his stare. Joe would see that silvery reminder of Jack every morning when he shaved.

Pure challenge marked Joe Sheldon's usually affable expression. Despite his almost casual tone, that confrontational air snapped in his eyes, stiffened his stance as he rose.

"Everything is fine," she hurried to assure him.

"He's not bothering you?"

It sounded almost as if Jack sighed. Or maybe what she heard was exasperation. "I told you last night I'm not going to cause her any trouble."

"I know what you said," the deputy countered flatly, "but I'd prefer to make sure for myself." One sandy-blond eyebrow arched in her direction. "Emmy? Is he bothering you or not?"

Jack Travers definitely bothered her. Though both men were the same impressive height and Joe was probably brawnier, it was the tension in Jack's leanly muscular body that coiled around her, making her aware of him in ways she truly didn't want to acknowledge or consider. Especially with the little battle of testosterone taking place between him and their local deputy.

"Jack is just here to take care of some...family business," she decided to call it. "We were just about to finish up."

"Do you want me to stick around while you do?"

That was the last thing she needed, she thought. "Thanks, Joe. But I'm fine. Really."

Despite her implied assurance that she wasn't being inconvenienced or otherwise distressed, Joe still didn't look as if he trusted Jack when he looked back to where he stood a few feet from the evaporator.

Behind Jack's big body, steam from the pan rose like slow, simmering fury.

"The temperature's starting to drop, Travers. That means the roads will be icing over soon. If you leave in the next ten minutes, you should be able to make it as far as St. Johnsbury before dark. With the storm moving in, I'd hate to find you off the road in a ditch."

Challenge worked both ways, Jack thought. Dead certain the man wasn't the least concerned with his safety, he met the warning with a flat, "I'll keep that in mind." He would leave when his business was finished.

The scar seemed to pucker as Joe's mouth thinned. Apparently feeling he'd made his point, he gave Rudy a final pat.

"You call me if you need anything, Emmy."

"I will," she murmured. "And thanks, Joe."

Her soft smile removed the strain from her pretty features, lit the little chips of silver in her eyes. Watching her, Jack saw that smile move to curve the lush fullness of her mouth.

The thought that the two of them had something going had barely tightened the knot in his gut when Emmy took another step forward.

"Give your wife a message for me, will you?" she asked, stopping the deputy just outside the door. "I have a dozen loaves of maple bread baked and in the freezer for the sugar-on-snow supper, but with the sap running, I'm not sure I'll have time to bake any more."

"A dozen loaves. Got it."

"And tell her Dora said she'd pick up the slack for me. I know Amber and she'll think she needs to bake my other dozen herself. Between teaching, heading up that committee and having a baby on the way, she has enough to do."

"You'll never convince her of that," Joe muttered, a hint of his good-natured self showing with his rueful smile. "But I'll tell her what you said."

The smile faded. Glancing over her shoulder, he shot Jack a scowl that made it clear he'd love an excuse to get even for the jaw incident, slapped on his hat and headed off in the falling snow.

Old resentments were surging hard when Emmy finally closed the door.

Aware of her unease with him, hating that it was there, Jack tried to stifle the bitterness Joe's posturing had brought.

Traces of it lingered anyway as he watched her head for the long work sink.

It seemed clear that she and Joe weren't a couple. Not bothering to wonder why he felt relieved by that, he wondered instead if there was any man in her life at all. He had the feeling there wasn't a boyfriend lurking in the background, though. The local deputy wouldn't have checked up on her so quickly had there been another man around.

"Were you and Joe ever involved?" he asked, just to be sure.

"Joe and me?" His blunt question stopped her short of the gurgling coffeemaker. It also had her looking totally baffled. "What makes you ask that?"

"I just thought he seemed kind of…protective."

"He's just being a friend. And, no," she said as if to end any further speculation, "we've never been 'involved.' I've never been involved with anyone around here."

She had just answered the next question he would have asked. He now knew for certain that she lived alone, and that except for the occasional help of an old man, she had to handle everything pretty much on her own.

He didn't like what that thought did to the sense of obligation that had brought him back there that morning. The fact that she was alone seemed to add another layer to that sense of responsibility, and tugged hard at a form of protectiveness toward her that didn't feel familiar at all.

"The Amber who Joe married." Still shaking the effects of Joe's little visit, he wandered toward her. Even as he did, Emmy moved to the steaming evaporator. "That isn't Amber McGraw, is it?"

"Amber's a McGraw," she confirmed as she checked a valve at the back of the pan. "Why?"

"Just curious." The bubbly blond cheerleader had been the subject of half the hockey and football teams' adolescent fantasies. Including his own. "How long have they been married?"

"Two or three years now, I think. She went to college

in Montpelier, then taught there for a while before she moved back." She glanced over to see that he'd crouched by her dog. Rudy had turned two circles on the red, cedar-stuffed cushion under her desk and plopped down to rest his chin on his paws. "I guess you would have all gone to school together."

"She was a year behind us." Jack held out his hand, watched Rudy lift his head to take a sniff. "But we went out for a while."

"You dated Amber?"

Relieved that at least the dog wasn't avoiding him, he scratched Rudy's furry neck, received a contented sigh for his efforts. "For a few months."

"It's no wonder he looked like he wanted your hide," she murmured. "You left him with a permanent reminder of how you beat him up, and you dated his wife."

"It was high school." His tone went as dry as dust. "She was hardly his wife at the time. And I didn't beat him up. I only swung once."

"And nearly broke his jaw."

Jack felt his own jaw go tight. "He called my father a bastard."

The quick edge in his tone made her hesitate.

"I'd heard you were looking for a fight because the coach had benched you. Joe just happened to be in the way."

"You heard wrong. I know I was mad because I got benched. The coach only did that to spite my dad. But I just wanted out of the locker room. Joe blocked the door so I couldn't leave, but no one seems to remember what he did or what he said. Not that it would have mattered," he muttered darkly. "I was my father's son. Once they'd condemned him, people wanted to believe the worst about all of us."

Emmy hesitated. "What about the other fights?"

He frowned. "What other fights? The only punch I ever threw was at Joe."

Emmy's immediate reaction was to insist that wasn't true. She didn't want anything to challenge the conclusions she'd finally managed to put to rest over the years. But Jack had already challenged what she'd believed simply by having come there. By what he had said about his mom. By what he'd said just now, and the quick, barely bridled anger behind it.

"I'd heard there were others," she admitted quietly.

"Well, there weren't. I've only hit one person in my life. And that was your deputy."

He had no reason to lie about such a thing. Not after all these years.

"Really?" she asked, anyway.

"Yeah," he muttered. "Really."

She could practically feel a corner of her old convictions crack. From Jack's knee-jerk reaction, it sounded as if he'd only been defending his father when he'd hit Joe.

She knew now that Jack hadn't agreed at all with his father's actions. And though she hated what his father had done, and while there was no way on God's green earth she would change her mind how she felt about that, she understood family loyalty well enough. If Joe truly had taunted Jack in such a way, then the man she'd thought of as another victim of the Larkins' destructive legacy might well have deserved exactly what he'd received.

Uneasy with the doubts Jack caused her to feel, she

forced her thoughts to her task. Thick steam was already rising as the evaporation process began, its sweet scent filling the room. It took forty gallons of sap to make a gallon of syrup. With over two hundred gallons in the pan, she had a lot of water to boil off, and other work to do before it became syrup. She still had to pack what she'd made last night.

A thermometer hung on the frame outside the multipaned window. Checking the temperature, she frowned. Joe had said the mercury was dropping. She just hadn't realized it had fallen far faster than she would have liked. With the temperature now below freezing, the flow of sap from the trees into the holding tank would soon stop, if it hadn't already.

"Joe is right, you know." She spoke as she moved to the coffeemaker that was on its final gurgle and hiss. She couldn't deny the conclusion Jack had drawn about the town having condemned them all. In her little neck of the woods, people were judged by their kin as much as they were by their own actions. The inhabitants of Maple Mountain weren't exactly the Hatfields and the McCoys. To the best of her knowledge no one had ever taken after a neighbor with a shotgun. But once sides were chosen and people decided who was right and who was wrong, it was easier to make a loon fly backward than to get folks to change their minds. "You don't want to get stuck out there. It'll just be a minute before your coffee is ready."

With the clock ticking on his departure, Jack jammed down the irritation that had slipped past his guard. Subtle, she was not. But she had a point. Getting stuck in the middle of nowhere was not something he wanted to do with a storm coming in. He did need to get out of there. He had movers coming at eight in the morning.

"Just answer one thing for me, would you?"

Removing the lid of a small insulated container, she filled it with hot water at the sink. "What's that?"

"What is it that we're being blamed for, beyond taking that property?"

For a moment it seemed her motions stilled. "I have no idea what you're talking about."

"I think you do." The sense of being wrongly accused battled the need to not sound totally insensitive. He already knew his own transgressions had been embellished upon. It seemed more possible by the minute that his father's had, too. "What happened to your parents, Emmy?"

This time, there was no mistaking her hesitation. It lasted a half-dozen seconds before she took a deep breath and reached to shut off the water.

"Dad was in an accident. Mom got sick." She set the container in the sink, reached for a white terry towel on the rack below to dry her hands. "What do want in your coffee? I don't have fresh cream out here, but there is powdered."

She clearly didn't want to talk about Stan and Cara. Had no intention of it, from what he could tell by her blunt change of subject.

"Black's fine."

Only a jerk would push about something so sensitive. Swallowing frustration, unable to imagine, anyway, how an accident or illness could be blamed on his father, he switched subjects himself.

"So, is it Emily or Emma?" It could be Emmaline or Emmanuel for all he knew. His jogging buddy's wife was

Saratoga. Sara to anyone who knew her, but that only proved that anything could be different from what it seemed. "And what's your middle name?"

The nature of her guard shifted with the slow shake of her head. "You don't give up easily, do you?"

"Rarely," he admitted, when 'never' was more like it. "So what's your name?"

"I told you—"

"I know," he cut in. "You don't want it. Why not?"

"Because I'm perfectly happy with exactly what I have."

He didn't believe that any more than he believed in the Tooth Fairy. Her hesitation moments ago had spoken volumes.

"No one is ever completely happy, Emmy."

"That depends on what they think is important. If a person is always wanting more than what they have, then they're probably not. If what they have is everything they want, then they are."

Jack didn't know a single soul who was totally content with where they were in their life, what they possessed, or who they were with. He had the feeling, though, that there was a certain sensible logic in her philosophy. He also had the feeling she might have just given him the key to her inexplicable refusal.

"So, you're totally happy. All the time."

"Probably not," she conceded a little too easily. "But I'm willing to settle for brief periods of close enough."

Leaving the towel on its hook, and the thermos in the sink to heat for a minute so it wouldn't crack when she poured in the hot coffee, she sought distance at the worktable. Picking up a roll of thin silver-colored elastic cord from the surface lined with log-cabin-shaped tins, she started cutting the cord into eight-inch lengths.

Jack stayed where he was by the pan. It was easier than following her all over the room. "'Brief periods' is a long way from 'perfectly happy,'" he informed her, watching her faintly agitated motions.

"Depends on your perspective. And, honest, I'm quite happy without that property."

"Have you considered what having it could mean?"

The metallic clip of scissors met the faint exasperation in her tone. "Have you considered that I meant what I said?"

"Have you always been so stubborn?" he countered.

"No," she admitted, still snipping lengths of cord. "I'm often worse."

"Emmy." Striving for patience, he moved to the table, anyway. "You're completely missing the bigger picture here. That property rightfully belongs to you. Just adding to the overall size of your acreage will increase the value of the land you already own."

"That's just a number on paper."

"It's an investment. And it wouldn't just be a number. You'll have more immediate income because you'll have all those additional trees to tap. Your revenue would go up by a third."

"My immediate revenue wouldn't go anywhere but down," she informed him. "My father was tapping those trees with buckets. I can't even afford to buy the reverse-osmosis machine I want, much less all the extra tubing and equipment it would take to gather sap from those trees the way I am from the rest of the sugar bush. Even if I had the extra money, I wouldn't have time to do all that extra work.

"Aside from that," she continued, quietly strengthening her position, "if I accept that land, I'd just have to pay taxes on it, and that would only take away from my income, too."

She had considered far more than he'd thought. Certainly far more than he had.

His brow pinched. "What's a reverse-osmosis machine?"

"Something that pulls water from the sap before it goes into the evaporator. Some of the new ones can cut boiling time by up to seventy-five percent."

"Then, lease out the land to one of the other sugar houses around here and let them boil that sap," he suggested, surprised that she wasn't seeing the obvious. "Or there's the big factory in St. Johnsbury. Whoever leases it from you can tap the trees and sell the sap. Either way, you'd have the lease income to pay taxes and buy your machine."

For a moment the only sounds in the little building were the muffled roar and crackle of the fire and the tolerant snip of her scissors.

"Edna Farber has a mule like you."

"Excuse me?"

"I'm not the one being stubborn here." She finally glanced up. "You're actually beyond obstinate," she concluded, studying him as if she'd never actually encountered a member of the human species quite so intractable. "You're not even listening to me. What part of 'I don't want it' do you not understand?"

He couldn't believe she'd just compared him to an old lady's mule. She even managed to look utterly angelic while doing it.

"If you don't want it, then sell it."

"*You* sell it," she countered before he could tell her she'd have a profit then, even after taxes. The man was beyond mulish. He was flat-out pigheaded. "I don't want the bother."

It wasn't just the inconvenience she didn't want. She didn't want anything to do with any money she might get from that land. No matter how it might be earned. She had no good feelings about the acreage that sat heavy with undergrowth just north of her modest twenty acres. Its loss had caused nothing but pain. She might have told him that, too, had she thought it would do any good. But he clearly wasn't hearing her more practical arguments. Since he'd brought back memories enough, she wasn't about to share an emotional one.

Jack frowned at the knot of restrained auburn hair atop her head as she started cutting again. He had no idea how anyone who looked so sweet could be so frustrating. He was also fresh out of ideas that might make the land appeal to her. He hadn't made it as far as he had by giving up in the face of a little resistance, however. Convinced there had to be some way to get her to take it, he was hoping whatever that way was would occur to him before she remembered the thermos when he noticed that a faint ticking sound had joined the crackle of the fire.

In the lengthening silence, Emmy seemed to notice it, too. The sound grew louder, turning to a clatter on the roof, against the walls. Looking as if she hoped the sound wasn't what she thought it was, she abandoned her task and hurried to the window by the door.

Chapter Four

The tug of apprehension Emmy felt when she opened the front door was familiar. So was the unwanted chill in her chest that had nothing to do with the blowing arctic air.

The wind she'd heard whistling through the cracks of the uninsulated building carried bullets of sleet from the slate-gray sky. Those pellets of ice stuck to the snow, the branches of the trees and were, at that very moment forming a crystalline sheet over the landscape and the roads.

As she heard Jack walk up behind her, it occurred to her that a sheet of ice was also forming on the freezing metal and glass of his car.

He must have realized that, too. He didn't swear. But the exasperated breath he exhaled made it sound as if he wanted to.

"I thought this wasn't supposed to hit until tonight."

She turned at the deep rumble of his voice. As near as he was, she couldn't see anything but a wall of charcoal-tweed sweater. Not needing anything else to unsettle her just then, she jerked her glance from his very solid-looking chest and turned back to close out the cold.

Rudy had darted to the door at the turn of its knob. From the click of his toenails on the floor, it sounded as if he'd decided he wanted nothing to do with what he'd seen out there and retreated to the comfort of his bed.

She envied her pet his oblivion. "That's what I'd heard, too."

"Do you think this has already hit the pass south of here?"

He needed to know if the pass was still open. Knowing an ice storm would close it, his question pulled her apprehension into focus.

Wanting desperately to escape that feeling, she cut a wide berth around him. "I'll check."

Steam and water vapor formed a billowy white blanket above the pan as she headed for her desk and dialed a number from a neatly typed list thumbtacked to a corkboard.

Snow was simply a way of life from roughly November to May and it literally took a blizzard to slow her and her neighbors down. It was freezing rain that she hated. Snow rarely damaged. Heavy sleet nearly always did.

She must not have been the only one calling the recording for the state Highway Department. The line was busy.

She told Jack that as she hung up and reached toward the shelf above the desk. "I'll try again in a minute. We might hear something on the radio."

Maple Mountain still only received one radio station. Jack swore it hadn't updated its programming in the past fifteen years, either. As the low notes of something that sounded suspiciously like elevator music joined the staccato tap of ice on the roof, he stood at the window watching a coat of ice form over the blurry landscape.

Moments ago he'd been thinking only of his frustration with Emmy's inexplicable stubbornness. His only thought now was that his schedule was in serious danger of being totally screwed.

His natural inclination to ignore what might slow him down locked firmly into place. He wasn't gaining a thing standing there wondering how far he could drive before he found himself stranded somewhere else he did want to be. What he needed was solid information.

"You have other things to do," he said, heading for the phone. "I'll try."

"The number for the Highway Department is third from the bottom on that list."

"Thanks," he murmured, and was thinking he would just hit Redial when he found himself frowning at the antiquated black telephone he'd only now noticed. The Smithsonian-quality instrument made the several-year-old computer on her painfully neat desk look positively cutting edge.

Picking up the heavy receiver, he stuck his finger in the rotary dial and placed his call. Except for the computer, the corkboard and the current calendar, it appeared she hadn't spent a dime upgrading anything. Though everything she used to make syrup looked scrupulously clean, her sugaring equipment was old, too. But then, he thought, listening to the ringing on the line, she'd said herself that if she'd had money to spare, she would spend it on a labor-saving device.

The recorded female voice on the other end of the line cut off his mental muttering. A minute later he slowly replaced the receiver.

"The recording hasn't been updated since this morning. The closures are all north and east of here." The fact that there were closures at all wasn't a good sign. "Do you know which way this thing is coming from?"

Emmy had returned to cutting lengths of elastic thread. Though her focus stayed on her task, a new note of disquiet entered her tone. "Northeast."

That meant the pass to the south was probably still open, he thought and shoved up the sleeve of his sweater to glance at his watch.

"It's hard to outrun weather."

Wondering how she could possibly have known what he was thinking, he glanced back up.

"As persistent as you seem to be," she explained, as if she'd read that thought, too, "I figured you'd think about trying."

At least persistent sounded better than obstinate. "There's nothing wrong with a little determination."

"As long as you don't confuse it with foolishness."

Now he was foolish?

"I have tire chains."

"They don't do much good on ice."

"They're better than nothing."

"And 'better than nothing' can be useless, too." She looked as she sounded, totally torn between the need to offer the warning and knowing what his heeding it would mean. "When it gets like this, nothing helps."

As anxious as she seemed to be to get rid of him, the

fact that she'd warned him at all stalled his request for sandbags or something to weigh down the back of his car for better traction. Conditions had to be fairly threatening for her to suggest that he delay his departure. That was exactly what she was doing, too. Telling him he really didn't want to go.

He moved toward the door but stopped at the window instead.

He'd already known chains on ice were next to useless. He just didn't want to concede the possibility that he could be stuck for another night. Yet, at the rate the ice was forming, if the road wasn't already as slick as a skating rink, it would be before he made it the two miles into Maple Mountain. Even if he made it that far without sliding off the narrow and winding mountain road, it would take another couple of hours to reach the highway. Much of that drive was through more mountains on roads that had already been snow covered when he'd traveled them yesterday. With the bulk of the weather front still coming in, he had no idea where he would be when it did or if the highway farther south would be plowed and open when he got there.

The wind shifted, driving pellets of ice harder against the building.

He didn't mind taking risks. A chance now and then was always good for an adrenaline rush. But his idea of a good time wasn't spending the night in a ditch and running out of gas trying to stay warm, or plunging down a hill because he couldn't see in a blizzard. He could barely see a few feet beyond the frosted corners of the glass as it was. Before long, he'd need an ice pick to get into his car.

He lifted his hand, shoved his fingers through his hair.

Watching his broad shoulders shift with the movement, Emmy suspected he was nearing the same disconcerting conclusion she'd reached herself.

The thought that he might not be able to leave battled the awful and unwanted fear that he would. She would love nothing more than for him to go and take the memories he'd brought with him. But if he did, the old and lingering dread that clutched at her even now would only grip harder. At least it would until she knew he was safe. She didn't know if he remembered the hazards of weather like this. But she was intimately familiar with just how dangerous the roads could be when ice slicked their surfaces. Especially on the curves. And the downhill grades. Her father had died on just such an afternoon.

The nerves jumping in her stomach formed a neat little knot. She had thought more about her past since Jack had bought that land than she had in the past couple of years. Wanting to escape the thoughts he'd elicited now, she quickly opened a box of the product tags she ordered from a maple syrup supply house.

"I have extra rooms," she told him, thinking the least she could do was offer him the shelter she would have offered anyone else in such conditions. Trying to ignore how torn she was about him taking it, she poked an elastic thread through the hole on the little pamphlet of maple facts. "Charlie sometimes stays with me when we're here late sugaring. And always when it's late and the weather turns. You're welcome to stay, too." Her voice dropped. "When it gets like this, none of the roads are safe."

Her offer made him glance back to her, but it was something in her voice that had caught Jack's attention. The odd strain in it almost sounded like a plea. Yet, all he could see in her expression was the anxious pinch of her brow as she concentrated on her task.

Considering who he was, he figured any anxiety he sensed in her was only there because she might be stuck with him. Despite her unexpected invitation, the physical distance she deliberately kept putting between them practically screamed of her unease with his presence.

Wondering how much more distance she thought she could get without disappearing through the wall behind her, he clamped down the fierce frustration clawing at him and, with one more glance toward the window, caved in to the inevitable. Nearly an inch of ice already coated the sill. He might be a lot of things, but he was no fool.

"Thanks," he muttered. He'd have to get on the phone first thing in the morning and call the movers. And his landlady. And his secretary. "It looks like I'm going to have to take you up on that."

His stomach churned at the thought of all that had to be rescheduled. Knowing there wasn't a thing he could do about any of it now, he did what he always did when the unforeseen messed with his priorities. He shifted to the next on the list. Or, as in this case, moved back to the one at the top.

"What do you want me to do?" A while ago, he'd thought he had ten minutes to figure out what was going on with her and Maple Mountain. It now seemed he had all night. "Put in more wood?" he asked, taking off his jacket to hang by her coat. He nodded toward the table. "Or work on those?"

Emmy couldn't deny the relief she felt knowing she

wouldn't have to worry about him going off the road somewhere. That relief, however, got buried as she dropped her tag to the table.

"I should have added wood ten minutes ago." Talking more to herself than to him, she skirted the table, headed for the pan. "That sap will take forever to boil down."

She couldn't believe how totally he'd distracted her. At least not until he stepped in front of her, blocking her path, and distracted her even more.

Suddenly faced with his big, very solid body, she jerked her glance from the slate-gray sweater covering his broad chest to the hard line of his jaw. As she did, she drew a breath that brought the scents of soap, warm male and citrus—and a sudden tightening in her belly when she met his eyes.

"Emmy." His deep voice dripped patience. "I just asked you if you wanted me to do that."

"You don't need to do anything. I can handle it."

"I'm sure you can," he replied, his expression mirroring his tone. "But it's either work or pace. Frankly, there's not enough room in here for much of the latter without climbing the walls, too."

The thought of him pacing from one end of the room to the other, all that latent tension following in his wake, threatened to have her pacing right with him.

"I remember how much work is involved with all this. If I'm staying, I might as well help while I'm here."

He had a point, she supposed. And what he wanted was only practical, given that Charlie wasn't there to help. "Three or four logs should do for now." Since his nearness did unfamiliar things to her nerves, moving seemed rather practical, too. "And a few more in ten minutes or so."

"What do you want me to do in between?" he asked, pointedly allowing her her space.

She motioned vaguely behind her. "Then, you can help tag tins. I need to get them finished before the first batch of syrup is ready."

With a little half smile for her concessions, he dipped his dark head toward the far end of the room. "Mind if I have a cup of that, then?"

The coffee. She couldn't believe how totally the man rattled her. Had he been anyone else, she would have offered it by now.

"Of course I don't mind," she murmured. "You wanted it black."

"I'll get it," he insisted, reaching to stop her, pulling back before he could touch her and somehow add to the fine tension edging into the confined space. "What about you? Do you want a cup?"

As jumpy as she suddenly felt, caffeine was the last thing she needed.

Telling him she didn't, thanking him anyway, she moved back behind the shield of the table. She'd thought she only had to make it through another few minutes before she could begin to put everything behind her again. The moment he left, she'd planned to turn up the radio or put a CD in her little player, throw herself into her tasks and forget about why he'd come and the memories he'd resurrected.

Now she felt the threat of more memories encroach as he moved about the room, putting logs in the arch, stopping to scratch Rudy's head, pouring his coffee. She was even more aware of the silence that followed after he set down his mug with the quiet clink of ceramic on the worktable.

She knew for a fact that she'd never been so conscious of Charlie going through those same motions.

Jack had stopped four feet from where she sat. She didn't have to look up to notice the speculation in his glance as it moved over her. He was getting ready to ask some other question she didn't want to answer. She could practically feel it.

"You look as if you're holding your breath."

That's because I am, she thought, her eyes on her task.

"Emmy." Tugging at the knees of his jeans, he crouched down to meet her at eye level. He hesitated a moment, then clasped both hands between his spread knees. "I know this situation is awkward. And I'm sorry to be putting you out. Just tell me what I can do to make you more comfortable with me."

She could think of several things that would help enormously. But it would betray more than it would remedy to tell him she would have preferred he be a little less insistent or intense or…male. She didn't care to mention that she'd prefer he stop messing with her nerves, either.

Figuring the flutter his nearness put in her stomach was her problem, not his, she offered the only thing he might actually be able to do something about.

"You can talk about something other than why you came here."

A tag slipped from her fingers. Reaching down, he picked it up, handed it back.

"That's it?"

"Please."

For a moment he said nothing else. He just crouched there looking as if he wanted her to pick some other means of conciliation before he planted his hand on one rather powerful-looking thigh and rose like a panther about to pace.

Taking his coffee to the other side of the table, he set it next to a wooden chair holding an empty box and nodded toward the rows of cans on the worktable. "Is that what you made yesterday?"

"Part of it. I made the rest into maple candy."

"Do you sell much of that?"

She couldn't imagine that he was actually interested in her little operation. But he clearly intended to do what he could to dilute her discomfort before it could escalate.

She truly appreciated the effort. Even if it didn't really work.

"A few hundred boxes. Sometimes more."

She had been up until two that morning packaging and boxing the little maple-leaf-shaped candies she shipped to kitchen boutiques and gift shops in the ski towns of Stowe and Killington. She told him that, too. And that making them was a time-consuming process, but her profit margin was higher than with syrup. The demand for the syrup was greater, though. Syrup was a staple. The candy was a treat.

He hadn't sat down himself. Wondering if he still felt like pacing, suspecting he did, she watched him pick up one of the filled tins. The design hadn't changed in years. The little red and white container was lithographed with windows, a door and snow around its base. The pour spout and silver cap resembled a chimney.

She had no idea how he managed to look attractive with a scowl.

"I don't remember your dad putting tags on these."

"He didn't." Looking across the sea of tins on the table, her glance collided with the zipper of his jeans. Wishing he'd sit so he wouldn't seem so restless, she jerked her focus back to her task. "I added them after I read that marketing research showed consumers were drawn by containers that offered more than just product. The silver tie and little pamphlet of maple history and recipes make for a more appealing package. And the log cabin tin is still the most nostalgic."

He nodded toward an open case of empty pint cans. "What about those."

"They're for people looking more for value than nostalgia. The regular cans cost less, so they aren't paying for packaging."

Those were the tins she would fill when the next batch was ready, she told him. So he started packing the tins she'd tagged, and then tagged with her while the room filled with sweetly scented steam and the sap turned thick and amber.

With the maintenance she would have to do in the sugar bush, she was easily doing more work than two people could comfortably manage. That became even more evident to Jack as the ice continued to build and they filtered and tinned batch after batch of the golden liquid.

Not once during that time did she say a word about how difficult it was working on her own. Or how badly she could have used Charlie's help the past week. Jack couldn't help thinking about it himself, though, as they went about the chores that were still surprisingly familiar to him and listened to the radio announcer track the course of the storm. It had reached upstate New York by the time the last batch was sealed and they'd washed and sterilized all the equipment they'd used.

She didn't say anything about how miserable the weather was outside, either, much less balk at going out in what alternated between heavy snow and a blizzard.

By the time the work of the day was finished, it was nearing midnight. While he banked the fire he'd kept going all night, she clipped on Rudy's leash, then handed him his parka. Lights out, hoods up and heads down, they went out into a storm that would have kept most sane people under any roof they could find.

He knew from having lived there that natives of the area tended to shrug at some storms the way others did a single snowflake. Winters in northern Vermont weren't for the faint-hearted.

The wind whistled through the skeletal trees. The blowing snow stung like nettles against his face. It wasn't cold enough to freeze the inside of his nose or the back of his throat as the air had sometimes done when he was a kid, but he'd forgotten about being in weather so severe.

He'd also forgotten about the system of ropes they followed with hands and flashlights. Those ropes were tied tree to tree and led from the sugar house to her back door. Farmers had used the method for centuries to get to and from their barns to tend livestock in bad weather. Sugar makers had used it for just as long.

It occurred to him as the cold rammed itself through his jeans, and ice cracked beneath their feet, that Emmy made this very trip every night for weeks in the cold and dark. Not in a storm like this, he reminded himself. But even with Rudy moving out ahead of her on his leash, he wasn't sure he liked the idea of her being out there all alone in the woods. There were coyotes and bobcats. Black bears.

Rudy would look like bait.

He'd already bitten back a dozen questions that evening. Knowing she was on her own, he hadn't been able to help wondering why she hadn't simply sold off everything and found an easier life for herself. She'd once had dreams. She could pursue them now. He'd hadn't asked, though. He'd been afraid he'd bump into something she didn't want to discuss and he hadn't wanted to crack the fragile ease he'd finally managed with her.

He was about to ask if Charlie usually made the trip with her when a blast of wind nearly made her lose her footing. Barely two feet behind her, he caught her against him, dropping his flashlight in the process. Holding her upright, he snatched the glowing light from the snow and slid his arm around her shoulder as Rudy doubled back.

"I'm okay," she insisted, inches from his face.

"I'm not," he muttered, and tightened her against his side.

Rudy seemed to have realized she'd nearly fallen. Thinking it good to know that she could count on her dog to maybe get her help if she were to slip and break something, if she didn't freeze first, he spotted the pale glow of her porch light through the heavy snow and angled them all toward the warmth of her house.

Rudy ran into the mudroom ahead of Emmy. Snow flew as he gave a great shake and promptly disappeared into the kitchen in search of his dinner. Behind her, Emmy heard the storm door slam, then the inner one and the stomp of Jack's feet on the inside doormat.

Pulling off her fleece cap, she shook off the snow clinging to it and moved ahead to give Jack more space. Outside it had seemed she'd barely slipped before she'd felt his big body behind her. She wouldn't have fallen. She didn't think she would have, anyway. But he'd spared her having to find out for certain when he'd thrown his arm around her and headed her toward the porch.

She wasn't sure which she found more disconcerting. That she hadn't minded how he'd ignored her insistence that she didn't need his help. Or the unexpected sense of safety she felt tucked against his side, his body shielding her against the worst of the wind. It wasn't often that she and Rudy had to venture out in such weather. When she did, she was never careless. She knew her way. And she was never out long. But that sudden and unfamiliar sensation of feeling protected had left her feeling oddly vulnerable now that it was no longer there.

From the corner of her eye she saw snow fall to the rug as Jack shoved back his hood and popped open the tabs on his jacket. Even though he hadn't brought up the property, it seemed there wasn't anything about him that didn't remind her of something she'd rather not think about.

Tossing her gloves and cap onto the dryer, she blew at a strand of hair that had loosened from her ponytail. He had wanted to talk about the property, though. She was as certain of that as she was of mud in the spring. She'd had the feeling he might resort to the pacing he'd threatened, too. Yet, he hadn't done that, either. He might as well have. All evening he had reminded her of an animal moving around a pen much too small for its power and size.

He still did.

She turned to the line of hooks opposite a wall of snowshoes, skis and the shovel she used on the back stairs. Jack had already shrugged out of his snow-covered jacket. His dark hair looked as if he'd just run his fingers through it. Against his cold-reddened cheeks, his eyes looked as blue as lasers.

"Just hang your things here," she told him, shivering a little as she toed off her boots. "I'll get us something to eat."

Knowing she really did need to feed him, she headed in her stocking feet for the warmth—and space—of her kitchen. It would take a fair amount of fuel to feed all that muscle, and all she'd had to offer him in the sugar house was coffee and granola bars. Considering how much he'd helped her, it was the least she could do.

If not for his help, she would still be in the sugar house. At the rate the snow was falling, she might well have eventually found herself snowed in out there, too.

"Will soup be okay?"

"Anything," he replied over the sound of a heavy boot hitting the floor.

She'd left on the light over the sink, the one that spilled its glow out the window and, on clear nights, led her back to her home. Flipping on the overhead lights, she moved through her bright country kitchen with its sunny yellow walls and maple wood parson's table in the breakfast alcove.

It should be easier being with him in the home where she often welcomed three couples a weekend during the fall color season. There was far more space here. More rooms. Walls. She could even think of him as she would any other guest.

She could try, anyway.

She was halfway to the refrigerator, intending to make a sandwich for him, too, when she heard his muffled footfall on her polished pine floor. Thinking she'd better get the other male in the room fed first, since he was pawing at his empty dish, she turned in her tracks and headed for the pantry.

The moment she did, the lights went out.

In the split second before the room went black, she'd noticed that Jack was only a couple of steps away. In the next second they'd both sidestepped in the same direction and she felt as if she'd hit a brick wall.

Her hand caught his arm. His grazed the side of her breast as it raised toward her shoulder, then suddenly landed at her waist. It seemed that her breath had barely snagged in her throat at that intimate brush of his fingers when she realized she was braced the length of his body. His thighs felt like hot steel against hers. Where his strong hands clamped her waist, heat radiated inward.

They'd walked right into each other.

His voice came from above her, its deep tones flowing like warm brandy over her scrambled nerves. "Are you okay?"

Her breath slithered out. "I'm…fine,"

"You don't sound fine." One hand left her waist. A heartbeat later, she felt his cold fingers skim the side of her neck before his palm cupped her cheek. "Did I knock the breath out of you?"

His gentleness was as unexpected as the concern in his voice. So was the sudden ache filling her chest. What she'd felt tucked against him outside had hinted at security, safety. What she felt now drew her even more.

It had been forever since she had been in a man's arms. Longer than that since she'd been touched with such tenderness.

It was such a little thing. But that touch put another crack in the shadowy image she'd carried of him all these years.

There had been a time when she had thought of him almost as family. It seemed that her father had. And, as a young girl, she had thought he must be nearly as strong and wise as her dad. And kind. She'd once thought of him as so very kind.

Yet, as his hand slipped away now, she sensed nothing brotherly or familial about him at all. And she found herself thinking of him only as…dangerous.

"No, I…no," she repeated, and decided to let it go at that.

Jack felt her fingers ease their death grip on his arm. Beneath his hand at her slender waist it felt as if the tension in her undeniably feminine body pretty much echoed the tension in his own. The firmness of her small breast had burned itself into his brain, right along with the softness of her skin, the freshness of her scent and knowledge that, were he to pull her closer, her body would fit perfectly with his.

Steeling himself against the tightness low in his groin, he slowly eased her back.

"Stay put," he told her, his voice taut. "I'll get one of the flashlights we left in the other room."

Emmy felt him move away. Easing out her breath, she took a step sideways, then another, blindly feeling for the counter she knew was somewhere beside her. It occurred to her, vaguely, that she could have told him she would get the flashlight. She also could have told him not to bother, that she could get one from the drawer next to her. But as she watched his shadowed shape return behind the beam of white light trained on the floor, she focused only on the need to get through supper and get him to his room.

Determined to hide the confusion she felt toward him, she turned to the cabinet beside her, crouched down to open it.

"Just let me get the oil lamps lit," she said, a faint strain in her voice. "Then I'll get your supper. I have a backup generator, but I have to turn it on outside. We can just use the lamps for tonight.

"There's a bathroom to your right through there," she continued, indicating the doorway ahead of him. "You can take the flashlight with you and wash up if you'd like."

It was as clear to her as the chimney on the lamp she set on the counter that Jack knew she was seeking a little distance. It seemed equally apparent that he wanted a little himself.

"You don't need to feed me. If it's all the same to you, I'll just take a couple of those apples over there." Shadows moved over his carved features as he nodded toward the bowl of fruit he'd seen on the parson's table. "Just show me where you want me."

Where she wanted him was in New York.

"If you're sure."

"I'm positive."

"Take as many as you want." He needed more than fruit. "Do you want some cheese and crackers?"

She had the feeling he was probably starving, but he told her the apples were fine. Not caring to push, she traded matches for the flashlight in the drawer, filled Rudy's dish with kibble and grabbed clean towels and toiletries from a hall closet before leading him past the hall to the stairs.

Jack didn't remember much about the old farmhouse. With only two flashlight beams to illuminate it, he couldn't tell if anything looked familiar or not as they moved up the polished maple staircase. His focus wasn't on paintings or architecture, anyway. It was on the woman moving ahead of him, the lightness of her stocking-clad feet on the dark carpet runner, the length of her legs, and the shape of her curvy little backside.

There were three bedrooms at the top of the landing. "Charlie stays in that room," she told him, indicating the one to the right. She turned left. "So I'll put you in here.

"I usually have the toiletries in the bathroom and fresh towels already out," she said, setting down the armful of towels on the foot of the four-poster bed. Atop them, she placed soap, shampoo and the other toiletries she'd gathered. After their third guest had come to her mom needing a razor and a toothbrush, they had started keeping them on hand—along with the toothpaste some people also forgot to pack. "I don't open for guests until the end of June."

He wasn't a guest, Jack thought. He was an intruder. As far as she was concerned, anyway. "Don't apologize. This is light-years beyond where I stayed last night."

Even at first glance and lit by flashlights, the decor spoke of a homey elegance he hadn't expected, and an attention to detail that betrayed a love of texture and form.

A faint smile curved her mouth. "Thanks," was all she said before she turned to a round, brocade-draped table by a tall wing chair and lit the chunky candle in the hurricane lamp. "Blow that out before you go to sleep, will you? And keep that flashlight."

She reached into a small closet framed with fluted molding. "There's plenty of hot water if you want to take a shower." Turning with a quilt that might well have been hand stitched, she set it next to the towels. "You might need this," she told him. "It'll get cool in here with the furnace out."

With a quick look around to make sure she hadn't forgotten anything, she backed toward the door, stopped with her hand on the knob. "Can I get you anything else?"

He glanced toward the bed, piled high with blankets, a comforter and more pillows than he knew what to do with.

He told her he couldn't think of thing.

"Then sleep well," she said, and closed the door behind her.

Walking over to the bed, he tossed one of the apples onto it. He annihilated a third of the other one in one bite.

Even as tired as felt, he doubted he'd sleep anytime soon.

He'd been fine while he'd worked with Emmy. Trying to figure out if it was just him or if she refused to talk about her past with anyone, he'd pretty much managed to avoid thinking about what he wasn't accomplishing being stuck where he was. But thoughts of her now only added a different edge to his restlessness.

He swore he could still smell her soft scent, that impossible combination of clean herbal shampoo and the sweet scent of maple that should have been too wholesome to be erotic.

It had been six months since he'd last been with a woman. His relationship with the female attorney he'd met negotiating a land sale had lasted less than a month, and he'd parted as amicably with her as he had most of the other women he'd shared dinner and a bed with. Not that there had been that many. He wasn't into recreational sex. But he wasn't looking for a permanent relationship, either. He'd never seen a good marriage. Certainly the cold war his parents had fought left little to recommend the institution. If he was going to do battle, he'd rather do it in a boardroom.

He polished off the apple, and carried the toiletries Emmy had given him into the bathroom. As far as the restlessness he felt tonight, he'd get over it. It didn't matter that the remembered feel of her skin and her shape taunted him even now. Making a move on Emmy Larkin would only add insult to injury. It wouldn't do a thing, either, toward getting her to open up to him. And tomorrow getting her to talk to him was exactly what he planned to do. Had it not been for that goal, knowing that he wouldn't be where he needed to be in the morning would have had him pacing a trench in her carpet.

Chapter Five

The power was still out the next morning. Jack's room was cold, and the battery was dead on his cell phone. He'd also had to dress in the same clothes he'd been living in since Saturday morning. The sense of frustration he'd wakened with momentarily eased, however, when he opened the door of his room and descended the staircase.

He smelled coffee.

That tantalizing aroma hooked him by the nose, led him straight into the kitchen. The room he'd so briefly seen last night seemed to welcome him with its warmth and the scents of something wonderful cooking atop the woodstove across from the currently useless electric range.

Welcome, however, wasn't what he sensed in the woman who glanced from where she'd set a blue-checked place mat at the far end of the parson's table. In the muted daylight filtering through the frost-cornered windows, Emmy looked decidedly cautious.

At least the dog seemed glad to see him. Rudy rose from where he'd curled up near the stove, walked over with something made of pink plush and missing an ear stuffed in his mouth and plopped himself at his feet for a pet.

Unable to resist the shameless bid for attention, Jack crouched down and scratched behind both floppy ears.

"How did you sleep?" he heard Emmy ask as she arranged utensils on a cloth napkin.

A desk and computer were tucked into a little office alcove just off the kitchen. From atop the black filing cabinet beside them came the low drone of a radio.

"Better than I thought I would," he admitted, half his focus on what the announcer was saying, half on the fact that she looked like a teenager with her long auburn hair clipped at her nape and hanging against her faded gray Maple Mountain Maroons sweatshirt. He never had been able to figure out why the football team had been named for a color. "The bed's great."

The compliment coaxed a faint smile. Or maybe the smile was for the dog that had just flopped over on his back for a belly rub. "Leave him alone, Rudy," she murmured to her pet. "Breakfast will be ready in ten minutes," she said to him.

She was going to feed him. He could have kissed her for that.

Pulling his glance from her mouth, frowning at himself for having let it wander there, he rubbed his fingers through the dog's thick fur to let him know he really wasn't being bothered by him and glanced toward the radio. "Mind if I turn that up?"

With her attention on breakfast, she motioned for him to go ahead.

Less than a minute later, he had heard enough and turned the volume back to a low drone.

Half the state was without power. Highways were closed. And the weather front that had moved in yesterday was apparently stalled right over them. No clearing was expected until later tomorrow.

The frustration he'd awakened with knotted itself in the muscles of his shoulders. The major highways would be the first to be plowed. Depending on how long that took, it could be another couple of days before they made it to a place as remote as Maple Mountain.

Rubbing the back of his neck, feeling a headache coming on, he mentally kicked himself for not having left when he'd planned on Saturday. He wouldn't think about how long he might be stuck. Not now. Not before he got some real food in his belly to relieve that particular edginess.

He turned to the windows by the parson's table. Emmy had shuttered her upstairs windows for the winter, so he hadn't been able to see what had accumulated outside. Already aware of a wall of white beyond the windows over the sink and near the mudroom, he looked past the frost clinging to the edges of the glass. Snow came down so hard he couldn't even see where he'd left his car.

"Would you like coffee?"

"Please," he asked, would have begged if he'd had to. "And a phone, if you don't mind. My cell is dead."

Emmy watched Jack step back from the window, and immediately pulled her glance from his broad back. Trying to think of him only as a guest, she lifted the blue-and-white-speckled coffeepot she used when the power was out from the top of the woodstove. "You can't get a signal here, anyway. It's because of the mountains," she explained, pouring coffee into two heavy cobalt-blue mugs.

Remembering he took his black, she carried his mug to the table. She would overlook the fact that she never served guests in the kitchen. She had no way to heat the dining room. When she'd gone outside a while ago to fire up the generator, she'd found that the battery needed to start it was dead. "I haven't used the phone this morning. But you're welcome to try it."

The implication that the telephone might not work made him ask if he could try it now. Telling him to go ahead, she returned to add milk to her own coffee while he crossed the room in his stocking feet.

The thought that she should ask if he wanted to wash out anything and dry it by the stove, or maybe borrow a clean pair of the socks Charlie had left there, was interrupted by the sounds of his voice rattling off the numbers on his calling card. Moments later, she heard him talking to someone about changing the time the movers were to be at his apartment.

She had finished toasting walnuts in a frying pan and had them chopped and in a dish by a bowl of raisins by the time he was on his second call. That one sounded as if it might have been to his landlord.

By the time she had brown sugar in another small bowl, cream in a pitcher, and eggs and sausage frying, he'd placed a call to a woman named Ruth who was apparently some sort of assistant, since he wanted her to reschedule some sort of staff meeting for him. He also asked that she book a room at the Ritz for a small reception for members of the Hilton Head project team next week, whatever that was, and to be sure the pâté was foie gras and the champagne Dom Perignon. He was now on the phone with a man he'd apparently planned to meet tomorrow morning to discuss problems with inspection approvals.

It wasn't like her to eavesdrop on another's conversation. But he was right there in her space making it impossible not to overhear. And everything she overheard made her think her initial impression of him that first day had been entirely accurate.

She had pegged him immediately for the high-powered executive type. As she listened to the deep, rumbling tones of his voice, there was no doubting the air of authority and command about him. He knew what he wanted and exactly how to go about getting it. What she hadn't imagined was the respect he apparently elicited from those on the other end of the line. It sounded as if he was put through immediately to whomever he asked for, and that whatever he asked for was granted without any question other than what else that person might be able to do to help him out.

It had been her experience that those accustomed to deference, the important—or self-important, anyway—were often demanding and impatient. Yet, Jack seemed neither. What she sensed in him was the same respect for those to whom he spoke that was given him, along with an amazing adaptability. He couldn't be where he needed to be, so he had just rescheduled what he could, made sure others were ready to act in his place in situations that couldn't be changed and, having spotted the battery backup for her computer and quickly asked if it could be used for her fax machine after learning her generator was out, arranged to have what he alone could do sent to him there.

She didn't want him to be decisive. She didn't want him to sound as if he could get his life under control with just a few well-placed phone calls. And she really didn't want him standing there watching her when she couldn't get the tenderness she'd felt in his touch out of her head.

"You're moving?" she asked, setting the small bowls of condiments around the bowl of old-fashioned oatmeal she'd just dished up for him.

"Trying to." His glance followed the plate of eggs and sausage she carried over for him next. "I've been transferred to Boston. My landlady will make sure the movers get in, pack up what I didn't get around to and make sure everything gets on its way."

Thinking it no wonder he'd been anxious to use the phone, she motioned him to the table. "If you have all that that going on, why did you come here now?"

"Because it was the only extra time I had. I don't know when I'll have another free weekend, so it made sense to come here now." A faint edge entered his voice as he scraped chair legs over the floor. "Once I got the property, returning it was something I didn't want to put off."

Emmy's back stiffened ever so slightly. Having just inadvertently stumbled onto what she really didn't want to talk about, she was fully prepared to change the subject when she turned to see him standing with his hands on the back of his chair. He wasn't watching her as she'd suspected. He was eyeing his plate.

It seemed it hadn't been the subject that had put the low growl in his voice. It was hunger.

"Where's yours?"

"I already ate. Please," she said, since he was clearly waiting for her to sit down so he could do the same. "Go ahead."

Chair legs scraped again as she reached for her coffee. Thinking she'd leave him to his breakfast, she started toward the living room to build a fire in the fireplace. She'd reminded herself yesterday that she needed to check the backup generator for the sugar house and the bigger one for her home. Had she not been so completely sidetracked by him, and had the ice not hit when it had, she would have recharged the battery and they'd have had central heat and lights by now.

She made it as far as the staircase before she turned back around, diverted again. She didn't want to be curious about him. She couldn't help it, though. He was the son of a man who'd labored in the granite quarry west of Maple Mountain. The sons of the quarrymen, along with the sons of the farmers and the sugar makers she knew, tended to follow in their fathers' footsteps. And while they were good men, hardworking, down-to-earth, and while one occasionally did leave to go to college and find a career in a city, she'd never known one to come back driving a car like the one being buried in snow in her driveway or sounding as sophisticated and urbane as the man clearly enjoying her food at her table. He'd already liberally dosed his oatmeal with raisins and nuts, and half his sausages and eggs were gone.

"Did you buy a house in Boston?" she asked from the doorway.

Swallowing the last bite he'd taken, he shook his head, reached for his coffee. "A condo. I don't have time for upkeep on a house." His brow creased as he forked another piece of sausage. "I should call my assistant and see if she can supervise when they deliver my stuff. And the property manager so she can have the bellman let Ruth in."

He had a bellman? "Mind if I ask why you're moving there?"

The sausage was washed down with a swallow of coffee. "I'm taking over the regional office there. We build hotels, office buildings. That sort of thing."

We? "You have a business partner?"

"Thousands of them. Stockholders," he explained, and motioned to the chair at the other end of the table. "Why don't you come sit down?"

Clutching her mug, she gave her head a quick shake. "I have things to do," Emmy replied, not wanting to appear any more interested than she already did. "I just wondered how you got to where you seem to be. With your work," she clarified, because she didn't think she wanted to know if the money his father had recovered from selling her father's land had been used to start him on his way.

"You get scholarships and odd jobs to put yourself through college," Jack replied with a dismissing shrug. "Then you get lucky enough to get into the master's program at Harvard and work your butt off for the best company you can find."

She had wanted to know, she realized. She also felt oddly relieved to learn he'd paid his own way. "You put yourself through school, then."

"Had to. My parents couldn't afford it."

"And you've worked your way up to…?"

Picking a forkful of eggs, he eyed his coffee again. "A vice president."

The man was clearly more interested in his meal than in his accomplishments. He didn't sound at all impressed with what he did, with what he had accomplished or with how far he had come in the years since he and his family had left.

"Your move to Boston is a promotion, then," she concluded.

"It's just a step along the way."

"To what?"

"To more. I wouldn't mind being CEO. Or president." Or both, he might have said.

Emmy blinked in disbelief. The man was thirty-two years old, a vice president of what sounded like a major corporation, undoubtedly had a lifestyle she could only fantasize about—and he wanted more. Not just more. He wanted it all. Since she never allowed herself to mentally venture beyond what she already had anymore, she couldn't imagine any reason for him not to be satisfied with what he already had himself.

"Why?" Trying to wrap her mind around such a huge dream, she slowly shook her head. "Has that always been your goal?"

Jack picked up his nearly empty mug. Watching her from the far end of the table, he saw curiosity shift through Emmy's unmasked expression. Her interest surprised him a little. The depth of it, anyway. That she came back when she could have simply disappeared on him surprised him, too.

He could tell her that he liked the challenges, the competition. He could tell her that business had become a game to him, and that there was nothing he enjoyed more than pushing himself to come up with a better strategy than the other guy. He loved the negotiations. He loved working with the germ of an idea and putting together the people, the land and the resources to make it happen. It would be the absolute truth. As far as it went.

"I like what I do," he said, going for the simple version of what consumed his life. "But, no," he added, his tone dropping as he considered what he hadn't for so long, "that didn't specifically start out as my goal." He hesitated. "My goal was what pushed me in the beginning, though."

She suddenly looked as confused as she did curious. "What was it?"

It was the very thing she didn't want to talk about. "Honestly?" he asked.

His glance swept her face, the sudden uncertainty in her gray eyes, the delicate quality of her features. He had a hard time picturing her as the child she'd been. The changes about her were too distracting, in a totally, nonchildlike sort of way. But the faded image of her holding her distraught father's hand had yet to disappear.

Rising to carry his mug to the stove, he suspected the interest she showed, however, was about to disappear completely.

"It had to do with what happened between our fathers," he said, and as sure as traffic tie-ups in midtown Manhattan, her curiosity died.

He poured himself more coffee, then walked over with the pot to where she'd stayed just inside the doorway clinging to hers.

"You asked," he reminded her, topping off her mug.

"I can't imagine how that had anything to do with the way you pushed yourself."

"It had everything to do with it."

He set the pot back on the crackling woodstove, set the potholder on the electric range near it. "I remember the last time I came here before we left," he told her, because that singular event seemed responsible for everything from his career to his being stuck with her now. "You were on your front porch with your dad, looking at me as if you thought I could somehow change what was going on.

"There was nothing I could do," he admitted, wondering if she even remembered what had haunted him off and on for years. "And I hated that I couldn't make things different." For her dad. And for her. "But when I left, I promised myself a career that was as far as I could get from running a crane in a quarry." And later, he thought, of running a crane loading boxes on a dock, as his father had done after they'd moved. "I didn't want to worry about hanging on to every penny I had. I wanted to have enough that if a friend got himself into trouble and needed help, I could give him what he needed and not worry about whether I ever got it back."

From behind him came the muffled snap of the fire and the low drone of the radio. For a long, uncertain moment, those were the only sounds to penetrate the sudden stillness as Emmy stared at the totally unpredictable man towering six feet away.

She didn't know what she had expected him to say, but it had never occurred to her that his life had been fundamentally affected, too, by what his father had done. It would never have occurred to her, either, that she could be so touched by what he had just admitted, whether she'd wanted to hear it or not.

She just didn't know which affected her more at the moment: his motivation to never be in a position where money mattered more than friendship or the fact that he remembered the last time he'd seen her. She wouldn't have thought he'd remembered her at all.

"I remember that day," she said, when remembering wasn't something she would have thought she'd care to do. "You'd come to give dad something."

"His truck keys," he reminded her.

"And you'd told him you were sorry."

Her father had wanted her to stay inside, she remembered. But she'd known their caller was Jack and she'd hurried out anyway. She had no sooner reached her father's side, though, than he'd grabbed her hand as if to keep her silent. Or maybe as if to safeguard her somehow.

She'd wanted to talk to Jack herself. She wanted to ask him why his dad had made hers so sad. Or maybe she'd wanted to know why he no longer wanted to be their friend. She wasn't sure now. Not after so long. But after her dad had said he was sorry, too, Jack had just looked at her, then turned around and walked away.

And decided never to be so powerless again.

She thought it ironic that she'd never imagined he could feel such a way. She'd seen him almost as a man back then. But he'd only been seventeen, and clearly going through his own torment because of Ed Travers.

In the years since, Jack had just managed to move a whole lot farther from his past than she had hers.

"I think my father would have liked your goal," she finally, quietly, admitted. She didn't want to talk of that time anymore, didn't want to think anymore of how horribly powerless she had felt herself. "I should let you get back to your breakfast."

"Yeah," he murmured. Looking as if a weight had just been lifted from his shoulders, or maybe just looking anxious to get back to what was cooling on the table, he gave her a small smile. "It's great, by the way. Thanks."

She'd barely told him he was welcome before Jack nodded toward the little office that might well save his sanity.

"And thanks for letting me switch the fax to your back-up battery."

From the way she murmured, "No problem," Jack had the feeling he could have wired the fax any way he wanted so long as it would keep him occupied somewhere other than where she was. Yet, even as she disappeared into the dim light beyond the stairway, she hadn't retreated from him as he'd thought she might at mention of their fathers. If he sensed anything in her at all, it was that maybe, just maybe, she was letting a little of her wariness about him…go.

In the few minutes it took Emmy to start a fire in the living room fireplace and sweep up the bits of bark from the hearth, Jack had finished his breakfast, stacked his dishes neatly by the sink and was on the phone in her little office alcove pacing as far as the cord would allow while giving his assistant her fax number. The woman must have entered the number even as they spoke. Emmy heard the beep that announced his fax coming in on her second line as she focused on the tasks of setting on a pot of soup for supper and washing up the dishes. The oil furnace didn't work because the fan that pushed the air needed electricity to run. But her water heater was propane, so hot water, they had.

Jack had hung up from that call, placed another and had just scanned the open surface of her desk and bookshelves when he turned with his hands on his hips.

"I'll dry those," he told her, noticing what she'd left draining by the sink, and turned back to her bookshelves. "I'm expecting another ten pages, and the fax is about out of paper. Do you have any more?"

"You don't need to dry dishes," she insisted back, and headed for one of the doors beneath her computer desk. Pulling out a ream of paper, she rose to load sheets into the fax's tray.

"I hardly use this anymore," she said, explaining why she hadn't noticed its tray was nearly empty. "Mostly I send and receive what I need online."

"For your sugaring operation," he concluded.

"And the B and B. The computers make running both businesses easier." He would certainly understand the advantages of such technology, she thought, also certain that what he relied on was far more sophisticated that what served her well enough.

"It actually makes the B and B possible," she admitted, sliding the guide back into place. "I get a lot of repeat guests, but most of my new bookings come from my Web site or the site for an innkeepers and bed-and-breakfast association. We have a tendency to take a little longer with progress around here, but there's no escaping some aspects of the twenty-first century."

Prepared to return to her task so he could return to his,

she stepped back and saw the green light blink on that indicated the rest of his fax was coming. "There you go."

"Thanks," Jack murmured, frowning.

"What?" she asked, thinking he needed something else.

"How long has the house been a B and B?"

She'd thought for certain his only concern just then would be his work. "About eleven years," she replied as that illusion slipped.

"Agnes said you'd turned down your scholarship to stay and help your mom run it." His glanced narrowed as he did a little mental math. "But eleven years ago, you'd only have been what? Sixteen?"

"I was fifteen when we starting converting it. It took about a year to get the bathrooms in upstairs and the rooms ready." Letting the scholarship remark go, she took a step back, trying as she did to move away from the past that had just sneaked up on her again. "I've had more bookings since I redecorated the rooms five years ago," she said, sticking to what felt safe, afraid that wasn't what he was after. "The common rooms, too. It's amazing what you can do with paint and a little fabric."

And a lot of reading, research and elbow grease, Jack thought, remembering what she'd told him about her interest in restorations. On top of the filing cabinet, a stack of *Architectural Digest* and decorating magazines shared space with books on Colonial and Early-American architecture. On the counter out in her mudroom were drawers from a chest she was apparently in the process of refinishing.

The money she hadn't put into the sugaring operation had all been spent on her home and increasing her profits there. He didn't know what she made sugaring, but depending on what she charged for a room and figuring a full house during the fall color season alone, the enterprise might easily bring in five to ten thousand dollars a year.

"So that's how your parents made up the difference."

"The difference?"

"In income," he explained. "I'd always wondered how your dad made up for the lost revenue after what happened."

She could let it go, Emmy told herself. She could go find something else to do and leave him to believe whatever he wanted so she wouldn't have to open doors she'd much rather leave closed. Heaven knew she didn't want to wander through any more than she already had. But Jack was proving himself to be a decent man, and it wouldn't be very decent of her to not allow him the truth. The simplified version, anyway.

"We didn't start taking in guests until after he died, Jack. Dad made up for the lost income from sugaring by taking on more odd jobs around the county." Her father had always taken on a few jobs in the summer, as much to help out a neighbor as to earn money for extras like an occasional vacation to the shore. But after he'd lost part of his land, the odd jobs became full-time and the extras had disappeared. "Once he was gone," she quickly concluded, "so was what he earned as a handyman. That's when mom started the B and B."

For several seconds Jack simply considered her. Or maybe what he considered was whether or not she would retreat from his question the way she had in the sugar house. "What happened to him, Emmy?"

She had intended to touch only on the surface. State the facts and let the details go. But it wasn't that simple. Not with him. He had asked last night what his father had been accused of beyond what he obviously knew, and now she saw that he deserved to know that, too.

"He started drinking after he lost that property," she told him, remembering how some people had said they could hardly blame him for that. Mostly she remembered how melancholy and distant her dad would become when he wasn't sober. "He knew the roads around here as well as he knew his own land. He knew how slick they could get when there was ice about and how easy it was to lose control. But he'd had too much to drink the afternoon an ice storm blew in and he got in the truck, anyway. He went off the road out by Sawyer's Creek bridge, and his truck hit a tree."

Crossing her arms over the faintly sick sensation the memory brought, she focused on the page slowly coming through the machine beside her. "Some people think he'd been so depressed since your dad sold that parcel that he did it on purpose."

From the corner of her eye, she'd caught the motion of Jack's hand as he'd lifted it to the back of his neck. Now he'd gone still.

His disbelief actually seemed to vibrate in the narrow space between them. "They think it was deliberate?"

"Some did. I imagine some still do." That was the talk that had always hurt the most. Refusing to dwell on that thought, she forced certainty into her voice. "I can't believe he would do that. He loved Mom and me too much."

The page fell into the receiving tray. With the rhythmic drone of the print cartridge passing across paper, she watched another inch its way out.

Jack barely noticed the pages accumulating in front of Emmy. Feeling sucker punched, he couldn't have cared less about what had seemed so important only minutes ago. He had reasons to challenge what Emmy believed about her dad. Good reasons. But it was what she had just implied about his own father that left him staring, speechless, at the side of her head.

She had just told him that his father had been blamed, however indirectly, for causing her father's death.

She had also just allowed a glimpse of what life for her must have been like during the three years before her father had slid into that tree. She would have only been fifteen when that had happened.

It was no wonder she'd been so anxious about the sleet yesterday.

Speaking quietly, because something about Emmy demanded calm just then, he made himself keep digging. "What about your mom? What happened to her?"

"She died three years later. Dad had been her life," she confided, still watching the machine, her thoughts seeming farther away. "Mom didn't seem to really care about much of anything after he was gone." She lifted one shoulder in a shrug that seemed to say, *Not even me,* only to quickly ease beyond that part of her past.

"She seemed better once Dora talked her into converting the house," she continued, referring to the woman who owned the community's only diner. "We sold what we could to finance the changes we had to make. Most of Dad's power tools and his hunting guns. Chaps," she said, speaking of her horse. "But Mom was always coming down with a cold or the flu," she explained, saying nothing about what the loss of her beloved mare had meant to her. "That's why I turned down the scholarship and stayed here. I knew she'd never be able to keep the place up for guests and handle the sugaring operation on her own." She reached toward the machine as it beeped. "The winter she caught pneumonia, she just didn't seem to have the energy to fight it."

Jack remembered Cara Larkin. She'd been a slender woman, much like her daughter. The difference being that Emmy, though she looked fragile, had an undeniable strength about her. Mentally. Physically. She would bend, but she wouldn't break. At least not without a fight. She possessed a quiet manner, but she was far from meek. By comparison Mrs. Larkin had merely been frail and far more docile.

As Emmy picked up the pages of the report he needed to review, methodically putting them in order, he couldn't help but think that Cara Larkin had undoubtedly relied far more heavily on her daughter than Emmy was admitting, then left her to cope on her own.

A quiet, unexpected anger surged silently through his veins. Anger at the locals for placing blame where it didn't belong. Anger at her mother for not fighting to get well for her daughter. Anger at her father for compromising his family. He didn't doubt for a moment that Cara's pining away had been blamed on his father, too. So that meant his father had been held responsible in some way for the demise of both her parents. And for leaving Emmy alone.

He couldn't help how people chose to point fingers. If there was one finger pointing out, there were three pointing back. Yet people seldom checked for skeletons in their own closet when they were busy building a case against someone they didn't like. What mattered most at that moment was the lovely young woman handing him his document.

Beneath his anger, he couldn't believe how sorry he felt for what she'd experienced, for what she'd lost. But he had the feeling that pity was the last thing Emmy would want from anyone.

He took the pages she held, set them next to her mouse pad with its bright yellow sunflowers. The quiet tones of her voice had remained matter-of-fact, and she'd kept much of what she felt about all that had happened locked away. With that same reserve in place, she now seemed to brace herself against whatever sympathy—or defense—he might feel compelled to offer.

"Do you have any other family?"

He watched her glance up, caution filling her eyes. "None that I really know. Dad was an only child, and he inherited this place after his parents died. That was before I was born. Mom has a sister in Ohio and her parents moved there after they sold their farm."

"When was that?"

She shrugged. "At least twenty years ago. They don't travel much, and I have a hard time getting away from here. I send them syrup, though." A faint smile moved through the caution. "They say they always look forward to getting it."

He still couldn't get past the thought that her mom had had to sell her horse.

"You know," he said, thinking it no wonder she hadn't wanted to talk about her parents or why he'd come there. That property couldn't possibly mean anything good to her.

"I don't know too many people who would have stayed here and taken on what you have. I don't know anyone who would have wanted to."

The expected defense wasn't there. Since he hadn't burdened her with sympathy, either, a hint of her caution faded.

"It's my home. My security," she admitted, her shrug almost self-conscious this time. "It's all I have."

"But what about what you want?"

"I told you before, I have everything I want."

"What about a family? A husband to help you out here. Children."

The look she shot him held infinite patience. "This is Maple Mountain. The only eligible men around here are either eighteen or eighty."

He would have asked why she didn't sell everything and go where she could meet some eligible men, then. Make another life for herself. An easier life. One where she could pursue the dream that had once been denied her and go to school. But the ring of the phone cut between them, relieving her of any further intrusion into what she undoubtedly felt was none of his concern, and sparing him asking what he suspected he already knew, anyway.

After all that had happened, after all that had been taken from her, it seemed entirely possible that she had attached the love she'd felt for her family to all that was left of them. She'd just said herself that her home and the land were all she had.

The call was for Emmy. It was Charlie, apparently calling to make sure she had made it in from the sugar house last night. Jack heard a smile enter her voice as she assured him that she and Rudy were snug in the house, then asked how he and his wife were doing and who else he'd heard from, to make sure her other neighbors were all right, too.

Jack noticed she chose not to mention his presence. He didn't know if she didn't want to worry her elderly friend or if she was trying to forget about his presence herself, but he didn't blame her that judicious bit of silence. News of a Travers snowed in with the only surviving Larkin would only add more knots to the already tangled grapevine.

It suddenly seemed infinitely preferable to tackle an environmental problem on a multimillion-dollar resort on Hilton Head than to think about anything concerning the good citizens of Maple Mountain. He preferred the distraction, too, to the slowly churning turmoil he felt with Emmy and the knowledge he had about her father.

Picking up his document, he headed for the parson's table since the light was better there, only to turn back because he needed a pen.

Emmy had apparently anticipated that. Her smile for Charlie still in place, she held one out to him.

With a smile, he left her to her call.

"You take care of that toe," Emmy said, over the scrape of chair legs and the plop of paper onto the table. "And thanks for checking on me," she concluded, before Charlie claimed it was nothing and she replaced the receiver on its base.

Charlie was a dear. As helpful a neighbor as a girl could want. Under any other circumstances, she wouldn't be feeling anything but grateful for his concern, and a little amused by his annoyance over how the weather had slowed down sugaring even though he wouldn't be sugaring, anyway. But what she felt at the moment seemed mostly to be the deep and distinct hollowness that had settled in the pit of her stomach.

The sensation was familiar. It was the void that had opened up when her father had started changing. The one that had grown larger when he'd died. The one that had become huge when her mom had gone. She'd learned to live with it, then to live around it and, finally, the awareness of it had faded.

The only reason she felt it now was because of the man who'd taken over her kitchen table. If not for him, she wouldn't have just been reminded that what surrounded her was pretty much the sum total of her life.

She normally didn't think about how she really had only herself to rely on. Or how, at the end of the day, she was the only human in the house. She adored her dog, even if their conversations were a tad one-sided. And she had wonderful neighbors. But they had their own families, their own lives.

She had no family. No children. No husband. She had no one to share with who truly cared about her. No man to just…hold her.

She could have cheerfully gone the rest of the decade without Jack reminding her of that.

Turning on her heel, she headed for the thermometer in the mudroom that indicated the outside temperature. From the moment Jack had shown up two days ago, he'd made her recall just about everything she'd struggled so hard to forget.

The thermometer with its little wire running under the window confirmed what she already knew from the weather report. Sap wouldn't be running today. Not that she cared to tackle the tail end of a blizzard to get to the sugar house, though she'd do it if she had to. As for the ice, she didn't want to think about that at all.

Desperately needing to be occupied, she headed into the living room. Intent on escaping all the unwanted thoughts plaguing her, she opened the heavy drapes to let in the light, added another log to the fire snapping in the stone fireplace and tackled the project she'd started before the flow of the sap had put a halt to her progress.

The carved wood mantel and fireplace surround was one she and her mom had salvaged from a house that had been razed near St. Johnsbury. They'd traded Jimmy Waters, Agnes's nephew, her dad's fishing equipment to help haul and install the beautiful old piece, but it had recently developed cracks. She'd filled them all in with wood filler but hadn't had time to sand or restain them.

By one o'clock she'd sanded the line of filler running the length of the eight-foot-long mantel, made grilled cheese sandwiches for lunch, stirred her soup and was back to sanding with a whole new set of unwanted thoughts nagging at her.

By three those thoughts had raised questions that demanded answers. Knowing Jack was the only one who could provide them, she was debating whether or not she wanted to interrupt his pacing in her kitchen when she heard him walk up behind her.

Chapter Six

Jack had never cared much for sitting still. Especially when he felt tense, stressed or restless. Battling all three, he'd paced while he'd waded through reports and dictated his replies to his new assistant. He'd paced during his conversations with a company attorney about an environmental problem and while he'd read through what his assistant had typed before sitting down to make changes and fax the pages back.

After that, he'd paced because the phone line had gone dead and he had no way to be sure the pages he'd sent had been received or that his landlady had let the movers in. He also still hadn't figured out how to set the record straight with Emmy about who was responsible for what with her dad. He didn't want to be as narrow as the minds in Maple Mountain and hold what she believed about his father against her. She could only believe what she'd been told. But he hated that his father was being held accountable for circumstances over which he'd had no control. He hated more that to clear his father's name on those points, he could easily destroy Stan Larkin's name. Emmy had lost enough without losing the image she'd had of her father, too.

Needing the distraction of work, needing more light, he'd just paced himself into the living room.

He hadn't seen Emmy since she'd come into the kitchen and distractedly prepared them both a sandwich while he'd been on the phone. Looking totally preoccupied, she'd left his lunch on the table and disappeared with her own, Rudy on her heels.

She seemed just as lost in thought now as he watched her sand one of the carved columns flanking the fireplace. With her back to him, her head bent, the top of her hair shimmered with shades of ruby and gold in the light of the blazing fire.

The floor creaked as he stepped from hardwood to the thick circle of patterned carpet covering the beautifully appointed room. Two pairs of burgundy wing chairs faced each other over an antique coffee table that held a collection of brass plates, candlesticks and a huge dried flower wreath that had graced the mantel. The tasseled throw pillows on the chairs matched the royal-blue paisley sofa facing the fireplace. Beyond it all an antique writing desk and mahogany-framed landscapes were centered between two farmhouse windows. Those tall glass panes, draped in that same paisley, revealed the snow that continued to fall.

Her hand fell from the column as she glanced toward him. "Taking a break?"

"Actually, I was going to get back to work," he said, wondering what had her looking so disturbed. "The phone went out a while ago, but I still need to review the last documents my assistant sent. It's just getting hard to read in there," he told her. "The lamp is out of oil. If you'll tell me where to find more, I'll get it."

Still caught in her contemplations, she set her sandpaper on the wide stone hearth. Brushing off her hands, she rose and started past him. "I'll get it."

"Emmy." His hands shot out, catching her by the shoulders. "I just told you I'd get it myself. You don't need to wait on me. Just tell me where it is."

He thought for certain that she would pull back as she had last night, step away as she tended to do when he came too close. It seemed a fair indication of how disturbed she was by her thoughts that she made no effort at all to move.

"May I ask you something, Jack?"

He thought he should move away himself. Her troubled question kept him right where he was.

"Of course you can."

Emmy felt his thumb brush the fabric covering her collarbone. The motion seemed almost unconscious, as instinctive to him as her own need to stay right where she was. That small motion and the weight of his hands on her shoulders reminded her of the gentleness she'd felt before at his touch—and somehow, suddenly, made the void inside her feel so much wider.

The wall of his chest looked so solid. His arms would feel so strong. Just standing as he was, just touching her, he made her want exactly what he'd reminded her she didn't have. It would feel so nice to be held. Even for a little while.

Realizing what she wanted, afraid he might realize it, too, she took a protective step back to search his eyes. There were more important things than not feeling alone. Right now she simply wanted to understand.

"Why didn't your father give my dad longer to repay him? I remember hearing him on the phone with your father." Before her mother had realized she was listening, she thought, and ushered her out of the room. "I know he begged for more time."

Jack had never regarded himself as being particularly empathetic. And he figured his sensitivity and powers of perception were as limited as any other man's when it came to reading a female's mind. Yet, there were times when all he had to do was meet this woman's eyes and he swore he could feel her tugging at his soul. He didn't care for the feeling. He wasn't sure he even trusted it. But tugging now from those smoke-gray depths was the quiet plea to simply comprehend what had happened all those years ago.

There were some questions he figured neither he nor anyone else would ever be able to resolve about his father. Or about Emmy's. But the question she'd just posed was one he could actually answer. He'd asked his mother the same thing the day they'd gone through his dad's desk.

"From what I understand," he offered, "your dad had agreed to pay the money back in a year. Two months after it was due, he still hadn't."

"But two months isn't that long," she hurried to protest.

"I know that. But when my dad found out why he'd borrowed it, he'd thought he'd never get it back. When the opportunity arose to sell the property and get his money, he took it."

He still couldn't imagine why his father hadn't even attempted to sell the property for more and given Ed the difference. He was about to mention that, too, when the auburn wings of Emmy's eyebrows drew over the confusion in her eyes.

"What do you mean, why he borrowed it? He borrowed it to buy sugaring equipment. Everyone knows that."

A log in the fireplace fell apart, sparks flying upward with the snap and sizzle of flames licking fresh pitch. The woodsy scent of that burning pine melded with hints of lemon oil and the cinnamon potpourri on one of the end tables. The scents were homey, comforting and had it not been for what he had just realized about Emmy, he might have considered how much more welcoming everything about her home felt compared to the hard angles of sleek marble, leather and metals with which he'd surrounded himself.

All he considered was the innocence in her expression. She seemed as clueless as he'd been about certain details of her father's life. At least, the details his mother had given him.

"Right," he murmured, scrambling for a way to ease back from what he'd said. He did not want to be responsible for taking away what she believed of her father. Yet, feeling as torn as he had fifteen years ago, he couldn't let the misconceptions she held about his father stand, either. "That's what I'd heard, too."

"Then you're not making sense. Your dad knew why he'd borrowed the money when he loaned it to him. What happened to make him suddenly think he'd never get it back?"

"Like I said, he didn't want to wait anymore. Your dad was already behind."

"But you said 'when he found out why he'd borrowed it.' If your dad suddenly didn't think he'd borrowed the money for sugaring equipment, what did he think he'd borrowed it for?"

The pleading in her eyes tore at him. So did the growing and unwanted need he felt to keep her from losing more than she already had. But she wasn't going to give up. As stubborn as he knew she was, he doubted she even understood the concept.

"Were you ever aware of a problem between your parents?"

"What does that have to do with the money?"

"Didn't you ever hear them arguing?" he asked, searching for some hint that she'd suspected problems existed. "Was your dad ever gone for long periods of time?"

"Never," she said, sounding utterly certain, and more than a little confused. "I don't remember them ever raising their voices to each other. Dad would come home late sometimes in the summer because his handyman jobs would be a ways away, but he was always home at night." She shook her head, shoved back a strand of hair that had loosed itself from the clip restraining it. "What does that have to do with your father?"

"What about your parents' relationship?" he asked, still searching. "Did they share the same bed?"

She gave a slow blink. "Excuse me?"

Jack heaved a sigh. "I just want to know if you knew their marriage was in trouble." She'd given him nothing. Nothing other than the sense that she had either been very protected or very adept at blocking all the things that had systematically robbed her of her security.

"My parents weren't happy, Jack. Our lives changed after your father sold that land. I asked Mom once why that made dad so sad. She said part of it was because they'd needed the money they earned from it. But what he really felt bad about was that the land was something his father had passed on to him and he was supposed to take care of it. Looking back on it now, I imagine Dad felt as if he'd failed his father. So if there was any trouble in their marriage, I don't think it was between him and Mom. It was because of your father."

"Don't, Emmy." The warning in his voice flashed in his eyes. "You're not pinning that one on him, too. The trouble was there long before your father ever even asked for that money."

"The trouble *started* with that money. If my dad hadn't borrowed—"

"That's not where it started," he cut in, cutting her off. "It's not," he repeated, banking the heat in his voice.

Moments ago he'd felt an obligation to protect her. Now that he'd been forced to the line, the obligation pulling at him was to a man he'd disagreed with and never truly understood, but who didn't deserve any more blame than he'd truly earned.

"Your father didn't borrow that money for equipment. He'd borrowed it because he'd gotten himself into a situation he couldn't handle on his own." There was no way to defend his father and spare her. Torn, the truth seemed more important. "He'd apparently had an affair with a woman he'd been doing odd jobs for, Emmy. They'd had a child together and he'd used what he'd borrowed from my dad to help her with her moving expenses and doctor bills.

"I understand that Dad asked him a couple of times why he didn't have the new equipment he was supposed to have bought," he continued evenly, watching her disbelief rise right along with denial. "Once your dad finally admitted what had happened, my dad believed your parents would wind up divorced. That meant your father would be paying child support to at least one woman. Maybe two. And Dad was sure he'd never see his money again."

Utter disbelief pulled Emmy from where Jack remained by a chair. It rooted her by the hearth, leaving her stunned and suddenly hugely skeptical of the man silently waiting for her to collect the thoughts that had scattered in a dozen different directions.

She had never heard even a trace of a rumor about her father and another woman. Not so much as a hint of speculation. Heaven knew that had there been anything to speculate about, the local gossips would have been on it in the time it took a snowflake to melt on a hot griddle.

"That can't possibly be true." His claim challenged everything she'd believed about her parents. Especially her father. She had adored him. And he had loved her and her mom. She'd never doubted that for an instant.

"You're just trying to excuse what your father did," she accused, unable to imagine why else he would say such things. "My father was a good man. A decent man. He would never have betrayed my mother like that."

"My mom is a decent woman, too," he countered, his voice remarkably calm for the defensiveness clawing inside him. "She had no reason not to tell me the truth as she knew it. She told me Mrs. Larkin confided in her herself about your dad's alcohol problem and about the other woman. And for what it's worth," he told her, giving the figurative rug beneath her feet another yank, "your father didn't start drinking after my dad called the loan. He'd been drinking long before that. If you want, I can even show you where he stashed his whiskey in the sugar house. I saw him taking hits off a bottle out there myself."

Denial surged. "I *never* saw him drink before—"

"You weren't always with him, Emmy."

"I saw how hard my parents worked to keep everything together," she insisted, ignoring his logic. "I know things were hard, but they never acted like there was anything wrong between the two of them. Not before they lost the land, and not after."

"You were a kid," he reminded her. "It's possible they were just careful not to let you see that something was wrong. Or maybe you just saw what you needed to see.

"I'm not trying to excuse my dad's part in this," he continued. "You asked why my dad didn't give yours more time, and I told you what I've been told. I didn't agree with the way my father chose to do things, but everyone has overlooked the fact that my dad had a family of his own to support. He worked hard for his money, too. You might also consider that my parents kept your parents' confidence. It's obvious that neither said a word about what was going on. With the way everyone talks around here, you know you'd have heard something about it by now if they had."

It was as apparent to Emmy as the muscle jerking in Jack's jaw that he resented the blame heaped on his father. Blame that had hung in the periphery of her own mind, and much of it unjust were she to believe what he'd just claimed.

Caught in a confusion of emotions she could barely begin to identify, she didn't feel at all inclined to forgive his father anything. Or Jack, for that matter. He wasn't the only one feeling offended. Aside from his impossible assertions, she very much resented his suggestion that she had somehow deluded herself all those years. He'd just implied that all she'd accepted as true had been nothing but illusion and lies.

She didn't believe him. Couldn't. But the last thing she wanted to do was deal with the latest developments from their fathers' actions in front of the man who'd just dumped them on her.

"I'm sure I never heard anything about it because it's not true," she insisted. She'd never understood why in less civilized times it often had been the messenger who'd been shot for delivering bad or questionable news. She now understood completely. "I really wish you had never come here, Jack. I wish you had just forgotten we even existed and kept your guilty conscience to yourself."

She saw a muscle in his jaw twitch a moment before she turned to snatch up her sandpaper. "There's a bottle of oil in the lower right cabinet in the mudroom. Matches are to the left of the sink."

The tension in the house became as thick as the blowing snow. Emmy managed to avoid Jack and the worst of it by digging out a box of old correspondence her mother had kept beneath the stairwell and closing herself in her bedroom at the end of the downstairs hall. Sitting on her white quilt-covered bed, she tore through those cards and letters by the light of the oil lamp she'd brought in last night and a high-powered flashlight looking for something—anything—that might verify his claim.

That was where she stayed until an hour later when she heard Jack, who had exiled himself in the kitchen, head upstairs, and the creak of the floorboards that told her he was in his room.

Rudy started pawing at her door to get out. Cold, because the closed door had blocked the minimal traces of heat in the hall, and knowing Rudy needed his supper, she hurried into the kitchen with her flashlight to fill his dish and set out some bread and a bowl of soup for the man who was probably now prowling his room like a caged panther. Every animal deserved to be fed.

She frowned at herself. She didn't want to think about Jack. She didn't want to do anything but prove to herself that he was wrong.

Fueled by that desire, she added more fuel to the woodstove and fireplace and let Jack know dinner was ready by knocking beside his partially open door. She didn't get close enough to see inside the dimly lit room. Nor did she wait for him to answer. She simply told him from the safety of that distance to help himself to the soup on the woodstove and to just leave his dishes in the sink. She was going to bed now.

She didn't go to bed, though. Having found nothing helpful in the box of letters, she quickly followed the beam of her flashlight into the dining room, pulled the old family Bible off one of the shelves of books lining the walls and took it to her room to search the entries her grandmother and her mother had made of births, marriages, confirmations and deaths. She went through the thick volume page by page, looking for a letter, a note, a date, a name.

She found nothing. So an hour later, after hearing the creak of boards above her that told her Jack had returned to his room, she quietly dragged out a trunk of her parents' memorabilia from under the stairwell.

For the next four hours she sat on the narrow hallway floor with Rudy curled up beside her, sharing his warmth, going through every letter, note, album and photograph by the light of the oil lamp she'd set above her on the small hallway table and the flashlight.

The pictures were the hardest. She hadn't seen any of them in years, and many brought memories that now seemed terribly bittersweet. Pictures of birthdays, Christmases, sledding and summer picnics. Picking berries by the creek. Riding Chaps. Yet what struck her most about those family photos was that her parents had looked so incredibly young in them—and that there were no pictures at all of the time after the property had been sold.

After finding nothing in the trunk, she took her flashlight back into the closet and brought out a box holding several years' worth of household bill receipts.

She found nothing there, either. Nor did she find anything in a box of old ledgers her father had kept. But by then her eyes had grown tired of reading in the eye-straining light, and she wasn't sure if she felt disappointed or relieved that she hadn't found anything the least incriminating.

Since she hadn't expected to find anything, she knew she should have felt nothing other than totally vindicated. Yet, as she left everything scattered on the floor and took the lamp into her room with Rudy on her heels, she couldn't shake the feeling that maybe all had not been as it had seemed. She'd found no evidence, but something Jack had said kept nagging at the core of her knee-jerk denial.

He had claimed that his mother had no reason not to tell him the truth. Considering that the woman knew her son's intent was to apologize and return the property, and that she'd believed at the time that her parents were still alive, making up such a thing would have made no sense at all.

The more Emmy thought about it as she hurried about in the chill of her room to ready herself for bed, and the more she tried to make herself remember, the more she realized that her mother had actually never said a word against either Ruth or Ed Travers. Nothing Emmy could recall hearing, anyway. Her mom had actually been strangely silent about them, except to say when she heard talk that she really wished everyone would mind their own business.

Leaving her door open to allow in the lingering heat from the other rooms, Emmy crawled under her thick quilts in her socks and thermal pajamas and blew out the lamp on her nightstand. Even as she did, she couldn't help but wonder if her mother's silence had actually been her way of defending the Traverses because they'd kept talk from becoming so much worse.

That same disquieting thought accompanied Emmy as she walked past her little mess in the hall the next morning. As soon she had some caffeine in her system to make up for her restless sleep, she would go through the boxes under the stairwell that she hadn't gone through last night.

Or so she was thinking when she walked into the kitchen intending to stoke the fire and start the coffee.

The room already felt toasty warm. Coffee perked away on the woodstove.

Jack was obviously up. He'd even done his laundry—last night before he'd gone upstairs the second time it seemed, judging from the pristine white undershirt and gray cotton turtleneck hanging over a chair by the stove. Both looked dry.

She could only assume that he was wearing whatever else he'd washed.

He wasn't in the kitchen. Neither was Rudy.

She'd just wondered if they'd gone upstairs when she noticed the door of the mudroom ajar. Seeing that Jack's boots and jacket were missing, she pulled open the back door and promptly shielded her eyes at the brightness of blinding white snow and brilliant blue sky.

Through the insulating glass of the storm door, her narrowed glance landed on Jack's broad back. He had already shoveled off the porch. Now he was working on the steps.

Her first thought was that he obviously couldn't wait to get out of there, though he was going to need snowshoes to do it. The snow piled on either side of the porch looked two feet deeper than it had been before. What occurred to her next was that Rudy wasn't pawing at the back door to answer nature's morning call because he was already out there with Jack.

Turning from the view of her dog contentedly watching his new friend scoop and toss snow like a man on a mission, she shoved back her hair and headed for the sink. The thought that she'd do the dishes he'd left there last night died when she saw that they had already been done.

It appeared that Jack had been up for quite a while.

It also seemed that he felt as guarded as she must have looked when he and Rudy walked in a minute later.

She had set a pot of water on to boil for oatmeal and poured herself a mug of steaming coffee when she heard his heavy footsteps go silent in the mudroom.

He was watching her. She could feel it even before she turned to see his glance run from the hair she hadn't bothered to restrain, over the shape of her face, her mouth, and settle on the pink fleece pullover she wore with her jeans and long silk underwear. Before she could do much more than note the sudden tightness of his jaw, he looked away to hang his parka on the hook and knock the snow from the bottom of his heavy boots.

The cold had turned his skin ruddy. Nighttime stubble shadowed his jaw. He looked more rugged than she'd seen him before, tougher in a decidedly masculine sort of way.

Clutching her mug where she stood absorbing warmth from the woodstove, she watched him move toward her. The blue of his eyes seemed as intense as the biting winter sky when he stopped six feet away.

The last time she'd seen him, she'd made it abundantly clear she wished she'd never laid eyes on him. The tension colliding with hers in the narrow space separating them made it abundantly clear he remembered that, too.

So much for treating him as if he were only a guest.

"Morning," he said.

"Morning," she echoed, hating the way the nerves in her stomach jumped.

"I did some laundry last night. Everything but my jeans." He nodded toward the chair that had served as a makeshift clothesline. "Hope you don't mind."

She swallowed, shook her head. The slate gray sweater he wore fit differently without the other layers under it. With only a single layer of knit covering his skin, she was more aware of sculpted muscles than sheer size. She was also aware that, with his underwear drying overnight, he must have slept in the nude and come downstairs this morning wearing nothing but the jeans clinging to his narrow hips.

The image that formed unbidden in her mind had her swallowing again. "Of course not."

"I heard on the radio that it's supposed to hit the high thirties today."

The weather, she thought, dragging her glance from his chest to her mug. She should focus on the weather, too. High thirties meant the sap could be running by noon.

"I'd better get busy after breakfast then. I'll need to dig out around the door of the sugar house and get a fire going. After this long, most of the embers will be out."

"I'll help you."

"That's not necessary," she insisted, thinking he had probably pulled on his sweater the moment he'd come down. With the furnace still out, the house was too cold first thing in the morning for a person to run around half-naked. "I can manage."

Feeling more in control having mentally covered him, she glanced up to see the telltale muscle in his jaw jerk. She'd noticed it jump that way before. Yesterday when he'd defended his father. The day before when he'd told her about what had actually happened between him and Joe.

His hands, raw red from working outside without gloves, landed on his hips. "Tell me something, Emmy." Challenge flashed in his eyes. His deep voice remained deceptively even. "Do you generally have a problem accepting help when someone offers it? Or is it only when I do?"

Puzzlement made her frown. "I accept help."

"From whom?"

"Charlie, for one," she replied, thinking that should be obvious.

"Does he work for you for free?"

"Of course not. He does a lot of work, so I pay him for it."

"I mean help you don't pay for."

Unable to imagine what he was getting at, thinking it best to avoid adding any more antagonism to what lingered from last night, she calmly said, "There's Bud Calder. He brings his wood splitter over and quarters limbs we clear from the sugar bush to use for firewood."

"And you don't pay him."

"Not with cash." She did barter, though. She did that with a lot of things. Everyone in Maple Mountain did. "But I do give him part of the wood to use for his family."

"I'm talking about just letting someone do something for you," he clarified. "No compensation. No trade. Just accepting a favor."

Emmy didn't know which bothered her more at the moment. The certainty in his expression that she preferred to keep things even so she wouldn't be obligated to someone, or the fact that he'd figured that out and seemed to have a problem with it.

Before she could say a word, he muttered a totally confusing, "That's what I thought," and headed toward the mug she'd set out for him on the counter.

"By the way," he continued, voice taut, "it'll be another day or two before I can get out of here, so I am going to help you. You've got two feet of new snow out there. The way the wind was blowing it'll be in drifts up to your head at the sugar house. If you're concerned about owing me because I helped you shovel it, just think of it as payback for room and board."

Mug in hand, Jack reached past her and picked up the enameled coffeepot from the woodstove to pour himself a much-needed cup of liquid caffeine. He wasn't sure what made him feel edgiest just then, knowing he should be in his office in Boston at that very moment, the fact that he'd lain awake half the night torn between regret and irritation with Emmy or having to cope with yet another legacy of their fathers' actions.

He'd noticed before how reluctant Emmy was to accept help. At first he'd thought she was just being polite in her small refusals. Or maybe that it was simply her nature to take care of those around her, no matter who they were. There was no mistaking how she tended to do everything she possibly could on her own. But he'd be willing to bet his new promotion that what some might see simply as graciousness or independence was also a need to protect herself.

She'd seen what had happened when her dad obligated himself to someone he'd thought a friend. After all that had happened to her, the thought of being obligated to anyone in any way might well feel threatening somehow. He could appreciate that, he supposed. Or would have, had he been in any frame of mind other than the one he was in now.

He took a sip of coffee, nearly burned his tongue. Swearing at his own impatience, he left the coffee to cool down a few degrees and reached for bowls to set the table whether she liked the idea of his help or not. He'd thought shoveling show would take the edge off his restiveness. And it had, until he'd walked back inside and seen her with her face freshly scrubbed and her hair tumbling in a fall of silk over her shoulders. As she'd stood cradling her mug, she'd looked impossibly sweet, incredibly sexy and, with the little sleep crease in her cheek, as if she were barely out of bed. Since thinking of her in bed led his thoughts in a direction he wouldn't let himself go, he turned to tell her he was going back outside to shovel until breakfast was ready—and found that she'd left the room.

The sound of something heavy hitting something solid filtered through the kitchen doorway. Wondering if his frustration had just worn through her commendable calm and she'd slammed herself into her room, he moved to the kitchen doorway and glanced down the hall between the wall and the staircase.

The three doors in the hallway were open. The hall itself was a mess. Jack had barely noticed the narrow hallway when he'd passed it on his way to the kitchen half an hour ago. With no windows to let in natural light, the space had merely been a shadow. The doorway at the end of the hall next to the bathroom was open now, though. So were the curtains on that room's window—her bedroom, he assumed from the black and white architectural drawings framed on the walls and the blanket and dog bone at the foot of a white-quilt-covered bed.

The bulk of his focus, however, was on what occupied the carpet runner halfway down the hall itself.

A large trunk, old and with leather hinges that buckled rather than latched, sat against one wainscoted wall. Surrounding it were stacks of albums, framed pictures, letters and a wooden holder of tobacco pipes beside an open cardboard box.

Another box, larger and looking far heavier, was emerging from behind a short open door on the staircase wall.

Stepping around the items scattered over the floor, he pulled the box into the middle of the hallway and crouched down to see Emmy on her knees under the stairwell. She'd set a flashlight on end, its beam pointing up and filling the small space with pale yellow light.

"What else do you want from in there?" he asked.

Emmy opened her mouth to tell him she could get what she was after. With him looking as if he dared her to do just that, she motioned behind her. "The two boxes on the far right," she said. "Everything else is Christmas decorations."

He held his hand out to her. Taking it because it looked as if he were daring her to refuse his help there, too, she let him pull her out and up to her feet.

With more ease than she could have managed, given how heavy the boxes were, he pushed them out, piled them atop the first box and closed the stairwell door.

In the daylight filtering in from her bedroom, she watched him frown at what she hadn't put away last night.

"What are you doing?" he asked, moving that frown to her.

Last evening Emmy had felt a faint sense of desperation as she'd first torn through, then more quietly considered the things she'd searched. That desperation had been masked by her certainty that she could somehow prove Jack wrong. With thoughts of how his mom wouldn't have invented something so outrageous, and her own mother's silence about his parents still fresh in her mind, she had the feeling now that she was clinging to a hope that might have no substance at all.

She'd heard nothing of an affair. But some of her father's summer jobs had been in communities far from the reach of Maple Mountain's network of prying eyes.

Still, she couldn't make herself let go.

Hating the doubts Jack raised, not crazy about him for planting them, she opened the box he had set on top and pulled out another of her father's old bookkeeping ledgers.

She opened the blue cloth-bound book, swallowed at the sight of her dad's neat columns of numbers. The ledger was for a sugaring season twenty years ago. She wanted those he'd kept for his summer jobs, but she would search everything.

"I'm looking for the name of the woman you said my father had been involved with." The sense of desperation didn't feel so masked now. Not with Jack watching her. He had a way of looking at her that made it feel as if he already knew whatever she tried to hide. "Or something about a baby."

Chapter Seven

Jack watched her turn the page. His heart involuntarily turned right with it. Emmy was no longer insisting that what his mother had told him couldn't be true, and the possibility that he'd told her nothing but the truth had left her without defenses. When she glanced up, she looked fragile enough to shatter.

"Did your mom mention a name?" The hesitation in her voice made it apparent she didn't know which would be better—having something solid to go on or still being able to doubt. "Or did she say what happened to the child?"

The restlessness Jack had felt moments ago had somehow deserted him. He wanted it back. Irritation and annoyance felt safer around her. Certainly safer than the need he felt to soothe the anxiety he'd so obviously caused.

He knew all about loyalty. All about the duty and need

to defend someone a person loved. That need was why she'd lashed out at him last night. That duty was why he had lashed back at her.

The edge refused to stay in his voice. "She didn't mention either to me. I can ask her," he offered, ducking his head to catch her glance when it fell. "If you want, I'll call her when the phone starts working."

Looking guilty for simply having the questions, she drew a breath, let it shudder out. Because she needed answers, she murmured a faint, "Okay."

He should go, he thought. He should go shovel snow and leave her to her search until breakfast was ready, then go back and shovel some more.

Watching her thread her fingers through her hair, thinking she looked either lost or overwhelmed or some draining combination of both, he stayed where he was instead. The little bomb that had exploded on her last night was the reason she seemed so terribly uncertain now. But he'd been the one to drop it. And she had been left to deal on her own often enough.

"Are you all right?"

Her hand fell as she met his eyes. "I'm fine," she said, sounding as if she were willing herself to be. "I'm just… I'm just trying…"

"Trying to what?" he coaxed, when she cut herself off with another shake of her head. He'd been where she was. He knew how hard the struggle could be. "I know what it's like to have a parent fall from his pedestal, Emmy." He offered the assurance easily, all too familiar with the conflicted emotions betrayed in her expression. "It hurts like hell. It leaves you questioning and feeling betrayed and wondering who you can trust if you can't trust one of the two people you're supposed to be able to believe in."

His voice dropped. "So what is it you're trying to do?" he asked, knowing the battle came down to two choices. "Are you trying to let go of the image you had of him…or hang on to it?"

Her eyes flicked hesitantly back to his. If he had to answer for her, he'd have to say she honestly didn't know.

He knew that for certain when she crossed her arms tightly beneath her breasts and her glance fell to the small patch of bare carpet between their feet.

"If what you said is true, then my father had been as much at fault for all that happened as your dad had been. And if my father was the one who started all the problems, then everything I'd assumed about my parents and their relationship was a lie."

Her brow pinched as she studied the carpet. "If that was a lie," she continued quietly, "their marriage hadn't been as solid and stable as I had always believed it to be. My father would have betrayed my mother." And broken her heart, she thought, because she would believe until the day she died herself that her mother had truly loved her father. "But Mom never said a word against him."

"I imagine she wanted to protect you." He'd suggested that to her before. She just hadn't been terribly receptive to anything he'd said at the time. For her sake, he hoped she was now. "They probably both did."

The haunted look Jack had remembered for so long filled her eyes as she lifted them to his.

"That would really be ironic." Her mouth curved, her smile as poignant as her sadness. "I'd tried to protect them, too. I'd just always felt I'd failed them both because I couldn't stop Dad's drinking or ease Mom's grief after he'd gone."

It was the smile he couldn't handle. That and the way she hugged herself as if she were the only support she had. With her arms locked so tightly, he'd never seen anyone look so badly in need of being held.

Without thinking about what he was doing, he lifted his hand and slowly skimmed the back of his fingers down her cheek.

"You didn't fail anyone, Emmy." He watched her eyes shy from his, felt her move almost imperceptibly toward his touch. "If anything, you were probably what kept them working together. It sounds to me as if your parents did the best they could to shield you from what was going on."

He didn't question the need he felt to offer her comfort as his hand slipped from the softness of her cheek and he eased her into his arms. He knew only that he needed to alleviate what he'd seen in her expression and that he'd do whatever he could to make it go away.

With her head still lowered, her forehead bumped his chest. She didn't bother to move. As if she were too caught up in her struggle to question anything herself, she simply let her head rest where it was.

"They'd succeeded, too," he reminded her, wanting her to focus on whatever positives had existed. "You were spared years of fighting and the stress kids grow up with when their parents' relationship sucks." He knew that stress. He'd been there, too. "They kept all that away from you. Think about that when you think about your dad."

Beneath his hand, he felt her narrow back rise with a slow,

indrawn breath. He couldn't believe how small she felt, how vulnerable. He couldn't believe, either, how much it meant when he felt her lean a little more heavily against him. It wasn't like him to give a woman the idea that he'd be there for her. But this was just for now. And this was Emmy.

Emmy eased out her breath, felt some of the anxiety gripping her body flow out with it. She didn't know which mattered to her more at that moment, Jack's surprising compassion for her memory of her father or what she felt locked in his strong arms.

She had wanted to be right where she was. She'd just had no idea how badly she'd needed the comfort he offered until she felt his heat surrounding her, seeping into her, calming her.

It made no sense to her that she should feel any comfort at all in the arms of the man causing her such upheaval. But the reassurance she felt was as real as the uncertainty still nagging at the back of her mind. It was in his words, his embrace, the gentle touch of his hand at the back of her head.

"It was never my intention to upset you." His breath feathered her hair. His hand slowly smoothed it down. "I know you might have a hard time believing it, but that's not why I came here."

Emmy closed her eyes, tried to blank her mind. She should tell him she knew that hadn't been his purpose. Circumstances had turned on him as much as they had on her. She knew, too, that she should move away. She shouldn't want so badly what he offered. But at that particular moment he wasn't tormenting her with some distant memory. He wasn't doing anything but encouraging feelings she hadn't experienced in her entire adult life. All she wanted was to stay where she was and let the balm of those compelling sensations wash over her.

With his arms surrounding her, shielded by his big body, she felt understanding in him. And acceptance of the neediness she would undoubtedly be embarrassed to death about later but wasn't going to worry about at all just now. Now she felt protected. And safe.

And not alone.

The feelings would be fleeting. She knew that. That was why she needed to absorb as much of them as she possibly could before those powerful and foreign sensations were gone.

"It's not," he repeated, his voice low as he smoothed her hair once more. "You believe me, don't you?"

From her silence, he probably thought she didn't know what to believe. She also had the feeling the respite he'd offered was about to end when he curved his fingers beneath her chin and tipped it up. Fearing he would see how badly she needed what he was giving, she looked away from the hard lines of disquiet carved in his expression.

His hands cradled her face, his palms cool against her skin. "Hey." With the pad of his thumb, he brushed along one cheekbone. "Talk to me."

"Yes," she finally whispered.

"Yes, what?"

"I believe you."

"Thank you," he murmured, and bent to press his lips to her forehead.

Emmy's heart caught at his unexpected tenderness. With his big hands framing her face, his kiss warming her skin, she could almost imagine what it would feel like to be truly cared for by this masterful and totally bewildering son of a man she'd thought she hated. Almost. The thought of being cared for that much by anyone seemed as foreign as every other sensation Jack caused her to feel.

She reached between them, slowly gripped a handful of his sweater. Swallowing against the odd tightness he put in her chest, she prepared herself for him to break that disarming contact. But he didn't pull back. When she reached for him, he simply carried that unbearably soft kiss to her temple, then angled her head to slowly cover her mouth with his.

Her heart bumped her ribs before her breath leaked out with a sigh. There was something in his kiss beyond the comfort he offered, something that felt almost like apology, or maybe it was regret, as he sought to soothe the aches and doubts he'd so unintentionally brought her. It felt as if he didn't want her to have to deal with the questions he'd raised. But as long as she had to deal with them, he didn't want her to have to cope alone.

The thought squeezed her chest even as her heartbeat quickened at the touch of his tongue to hers.

Slipping his arms around her, he drew her closer. His thighs brushed hers. His chest pressed against her fist. She was suddenly aware of little beyond his warmth moving into her, through her and touching a part of her that had felt so cold for so very long.

Her fist uncurled. Reaching up, she curved her arms around his neck, leaned closer still. That honeyed warmth drew her like fire on a freezing night. She needed to be closer. Needed more of his heat. Needed more of whatever else he could cause her to feel.

A faint moan came from deep in her chest. Or maybe, Jack thought, feeling her stretch her curvy little body against his, that low sound had been his own.

He was in trouble here. When he'd reached for her, his only thought had been to comfort. He'd never intended to do anything other than hold her. But that was before he'd been drawn by the softness of her skin, her sigh, and kissing her had suddenly seemed like the most natural thing in the world.

Holding her now, molding her body to his as she pressed closer, his thoughts had little to do with easing her mind and everything to do with the slow-burning hunger growing low in his gut.

She wanted this. She was seeking him as he now sought her.

The knowledge stunned him. It also threatened to override his common sense as his hand slipped beneath her soft shirt and over the satiny fabric covering her back. She tasted warm and sweet, like some exotic liquor that seemed innocent enough at first sip but slowly worked its way into a man's blood, heating it, hazing his mind. She tasted a little desperate, too, as she rose on tiptoe, kissing him back.

He caught the silk of her hair in his other hand, drank more deeply. Her mouth felt impossibly soft beneath his. The almost tentative touch of her tongue felt incredibly erotic. Each breath he drew brought the fresh, powdery scent of her into his lungs, heating the desire coursing through his blood. But no matter that she seemed so willing, no matter how unbelievably tempting he found her, she was forbidden fruit as far as he was concerned.

His heart felt as if it were about to pound out of his chest when he slipped his hands up to frame her face once more.

Edging her back, he rested his forehead against hers. Had they met under different circumstances, had he not come intending to close the book where their families were concerned, he suspected he wouldn't have kept his hands to himself even as long as he had. She was an intelligent, remarkable and beautiful woman, and right now he wanted her in bed, naked and moving beneath him. But sex with her would only add another layer of complications to their situation. And their situation felt complicated enough as it was.

"You know something, Emmy?" he asked, his voice husky with denied need. "I think I'd better get out of here before I change my mind."

Emmy's arms slipped back around herself. With her pulse scrambling, her knees weak, she edged back far enough to see the little cleft in his chin when he lifted his head. Shocked by how she'd craved his touch, embarrassed by how desperately she'd encouraged it, she blinked at his broad chest. "About what?"

"About behaving myself."

Embarrassment turned to something confusing, and terribly seductive, when he slipped his fingers beneath her chin and smoothed his moisture from her lower lip with his thumb.

"I'm going to start shoveling out around the sugar house," he told her, his focus on her mouth, his thoughts drifting toward stuffing snow in his pants. "How long do I have until breakfast?"

Emmy gave him twenty minutes, every one of which she spent vacillating between wishing he hadn't behaved himself and telling herself she should be grateful that he had.

She wasn't terribly experienced where men were concerned. Not intimately, anyway. She had male friends. Old ones. Young ones. A few in between. Two of those friends were boys, now men, she'd dated in high school. Rob Higgins, who ran a cattle and wheat ranch with his father, had taken her to homecoming and football games and taught her how to kiss. T.J. McGraw, whose mom still taught English and Home Ec., had taken her to the prom and been too shy to do anything other than hold her hand.

Both men were now married to women she shared recipes and committee projects with and who knew about the kissing and the handholding because they'd been in high school with her. But her only adult relationship had been with an English professor who'd stayed at her B and B four summers ago.

Jeremy Barton, Ph.D., had stayed from June until September writing a dissertation to be published in some collegiate tome that would ensure his professional immortality. He'd been young, smart and the biggest flirt she'd ever met, which should have been her first clue that she shouldn't take anything he said seriously—especially when he'd confided one summer evening that he'd become totally infatuated with her and Vermont.

Looking back, she supposed her only excuse for having been so easily seduced was because she'd lacked the sophistication to spot the human version of a tomcat. As she'd told Jack, the eligible men in Maple Mountain were either eighteen or eighty and at twenty-three, her experience had been sorely limited. As her business had grown, she'd since encountered other more urbane men from down country. But until Jeremy, no man had ever paid her the compliments or attention he had. She'd never opened up to him the way she had to Jack about her family, but she'd liked being with him because he'd given her something new to look forward to each morning.

He had also left exactly as scheduled—and she hadn't heard from him since.

Jack would leave, too.

Unfortunately, knowing that Jack would soon be gone did nothing to alleviate the pull she felt toward him. She knew her ability to confide in him existed mostly because they shared a history. He hadn't been around for the aftermath of his dad's decision, but he'd been there in the beginning and he'd known her mom and dad. Yet, that ability to share with him aside, no man had ever made her feel the raw need he had elicited. Or given her the sense that he cared about how his actions might affect her.

Still, Jack would leave. Being the practical person she was, Emmy figured that meant she didn't need to worry too much about why that pull was there. Or the undeniable strength of it. As she searched out a scrunchee and scraped her hair into a ponytail on the way into the kitchen, she had more immediate matters to tend. She needed to get them both fed, find her father's old snowshoes for Jack to use—the ones she hadn't wanted to sell because they'd belonged to her grandfather—and tackle the snow herself.

By one o'clock the icicles dangling from the eaves of the sugar house had started to slowly drip from the warmth of the sun. With the new layer of snow coating the roof and the branches of the trees glistening with snow-glazed ice, the world looked like something enchanted, something magical. A fairy forest, Emmy had called the winter woods as a child, because as a child, her imagination had run to all manner of fanciful things. Tiny fairies in glittering gowns of white frost and gossamer wings seemed to fit those fancies perfectly. She would even imagine that the diamondlike reflections of the sun sparkling on ice were those tiny, ephemeral spirits and make a wish before they shimmered away.

Watching the sun glitter on the ice coating a maple tree as she stood in the doorway of the sugar house, Emmy didn't notice any of that magic. As she had so often in her life, she simply felt as if she were holding her breath.

One of the tree's branches was broken. So were several others in the trees beyond. There hadn't been time yet to see what other damage had been done in the sugar bush.

"What's the matter?"

Emmy felt Jack stop behind her in the doorway of the sugar house. They had shoveled the five-foot-high drifts of snow from the window and doors, including the big one they'd had to open to bring in more wood. They'd shoveled around the woodshed, too, and brought in another load of split logs by dragging a loaded skid with the snowmobile Jack had retrieved from her converted stable. The machine had bogged down a couple of times in the drifts and they'd had to dig it out, but using it to pull the skid had still been easier than carrying all that wood through the snow themselves.

Everything was finally ready to start boiling. Would be when she started the fire, anyway. All she need was sap.

"I just checked the tank again," she replied. "There's nothing there yet."

Still hoping for the best, trying not to fear the worst, she moved to the next task on her mental list. "I need to let Rudy out for a minute." As much as her pet loved the outdoors, he didn't do well in fresh snow as deep as he was tall. An Alaskan husky, he was not. "We can bring lunch back here." Then, she thought, if there wasn't something in the tank, she would start checking the lines.

The small smile she gave Jack when she glanced up at him looked as distracted as he knew she was. She was worried. Worried and trying very hard not to let it show.

He'd seen the way she'd looked at the trees as they'd shoveled, and how her glance kept straying up the hills and into the woods. Some of the waist-high plastic pipelines still hung above the snow. Other lines were buried in drifts of the deep white stuff. A few broken branches dangled here and there.

Her eyes had met his when she'd first noticed those hints of larger damage, but she'd said nothing. Neither had he. They could only do one job at a time.

"Maybe the ice is keeping the trees from warming."

"Maybe," she murmured.

With a small, hopeful smile, she stepped outside to clamp on the snowshoes she'd stuck tail-end in the snow. Closing the door behind him, Jack moved beside her and strapped on the teardrop-shaped footgear that kept him from sinking to his knees with every step.

The fog of their breath trailed off in the crisp clean air as they started toward the house. Snow crunched beneath their feet, the only sound in the surrounding stillness. Since those unexpected moments in the hallway, a quiet sort of caution had slipped between them. It had been there as they'd dug and hauled. It lingered even now.

From the corner of her eye, Emmy saw him reach down and scoop up a handful of snow. Straightening, he let it filter through his bare fingers. Once they'd been able to get into the sugar house, he'd worn Charlie's old gloves from the woodpile while he'd worked. The leather was worn and uninsulated and would provide scant protection in real cold, but they were the only ones she had that were big enough for him to use.

"I forgot what it's like here after a storm."

She pulled her glance to the tracks they'd made in the snow that morning. He had good hands. Big. Strong. Capable. "It snows in the city."

"Not like this. It doesn't look like this for long, either. What isn't shoveled away, turns to a gritty slush along the curbs in a matter of hours."

"What about Central Park?" she asked, thinking of pictures she'd seen of its lawns and gardens. "Or Rockefeller Plaza?"

"Maybe not there." Tipping back his head, he looked up through the crystalline branches of the trees stretched across the azure sky. "But I've never been anywhere in a city where it's this quiet."

There was a special quiet in the deep woods. A profound sort of silence that somehow made all other senses sharper, more acute. Especially after a new snow. Cold felt crisper. Eyes seemed to catch movements that might have gone unnoticed. The quick flash of a doe darting through the trees. A flurry of snow silently falling from a bough, unweighting it, springing it back in place. That quiet could be so intense that it absorbed any trace of sound around it. So quiet it even seemed to muffle anxious thoughts.

The thought that Jack recalled that silence made her wonder if he might actually miss the place he'd left so long ago. Until just then, it hadn't occurred to her that he might have any pleasant memories of Maple Mountain at all.

"It's always like this here," she reminded him. "Even in the summer."

"Except for the birds."

"Did you like living here?" she asked, suddenly wanting to know. "Before, I mean."

A faint smile formed. "I was born here. What else did I know?"

"Is that a yes or no?"

Beneath his heavy parka, his broad shoulders lifted in a shrug. "There are a few things around here that I remember being pretty cool. Hanging out at the old mill. Skiing over at Hunter's Hill. Swimming out at the lake."

"What about the quiet? Do you miss it?"

He gave the matter a full six seconds' worth of thought. "Sometimes. But after a while, I think all the stillness would drive me nuts. I like the energy of a city." He brushed the remaining snow from his hands, wiped them against his jeans. "I like being close to restaurants and airports and in the middle of what's going on."

Emmy lifted her chin in acknowledgment. She would like the energy of the city, too, she thought. She just couldn't imagine living any way other than how she'd lived all of her life. She'd stopped trying to imagine when she was eighteen.

As for the quiet, that hushed stillness slowly faded with the encroaching whine of a snowmobile engine.

Two engines, Emmy realized as she and Jack emerged from the trees and the sounds grew louder.

Within seconds the vehicles came into sight, their riders bundled in snowmobile suits and helmets with face shields that totally obscured their identity. Despite the camouflage, she easily recognized her company.

From the sudden set to Jack's jaw, it seemed he had no trouble identifying one of them, either. Watching the two low-slung vehicles, one blue, the other black and bearing the crest of the county Sheriff's Department on its nose power toward them, he muttered a flat, "Great."

The roar of the machines all but drowned the terse sentiment, then eased off to a low, reverberating idle when both came to a stop ten feet ahead of where they'd stopped themselves. With the almost simultaneous turn of ignition keys, the engines died.

Joe dismounted first. Wearing a brown uniform snowmobile suit with Sheriff's Department insignia on the shoulder and his badge on his chest, he swung his leg over the seat like a ranger climbing off his horse. He'd no sooner removed his shiny helmet, than he bounced a glance of cautious censure between her and the man who'd just stopped at her side.

"I thought you left," he said to Jack. "Is everything okay here?" he immediately asked Emmy.

Intent on defusing the quick snap of tension in the cold air, Emmy offered a quiet, "Everything is fine. It started sleeting before Jack could get out of here, so I offered him a room. How is everyone else doing?" she asked, genuinely concerned. "No one got caught in the storm, I hope."

Joe distractedly rubbed his jaw. "Haven't been able to check on everybody yet. But so far, so good."

Relieved to hear that, she smiled past his shoulder. "Hi, Charlie," she said as the rider in the navy snowmobile suit dismounted with a little less ease than his companion.

Charlie Moorehouse removed his helmet to reveal a shock of silver hair and the full silver beard he grew every winter so he could play Santa at the community center. Grumpy as he'd grown to be in the past few years, his eyes still twinkled when he donned the red garb. He made an excellent Santa, too. He just required a lot of padding. The seventy-something ex-maple farmer was as tall and thin as a birch sapling.

"Is your toe better?" she asked.

Charlie was far from verbose. He also wasn't given to snap decisions.

"Uh," he began, scratching his beard. "Yup," he concluded, and sat himself sideways on the long black seat of his machine to hold up one foot. "Got a boot on."

"Charlie said he checked on you yesterday morning." His tone oddly accusing, Joe nodded toward the man who'd given him his scar. "You should have told him this guy was still here. We could have found a way to get him to the motel."

"I'm fine right where I am."

At Jack's flat statement, Joe's eyes narrowed. "I wasn't thinking of your comfort, Travers. I was thinking of how awkward it must be for Emmy to have to put you up and feed you. After what your father did to her family, she shouldn't have to —"

"Don't, Joe." The warning in Emmy's voice sounded suspiciously like the warning she'd heard in Jack's tone yesterday when she stepped on that same sensitive ground.

The fact that she spoke with warning at all had Joe and Jack both looking at her as if she'd just taken leave of her senses.

Still sitting sideways on his snowmobile, Charlie merely arched a bushy gray eyebrow at them all.

"Jack came to apologize for what his dad did," she told the scowling deputy, "and to return the land his father sold." It wasn't like her to share her personal business. But Jack didn't deserve the animosity Joe wasn't bothering to temper. Just as he hadn't deserved the coolness she'd first treated him with herself. "He isn't Ed Travers. So, please stop treating him like he is."

The deputy's square-jawed features folded into a deeper frown. She just wasn't sure what that frown was for—that Jack's purpose for darkening Maple Mountain's figurative doorstep was possibly honorable or that she had just defended the man.

From the low growl of his voice, she figured it was a little of both.

"He and I have our own issues, Emmy."

"We only have one," Jack muttered. "You're pissed because I hit you."

"You're damn right I am."

"Well, you're just going to have to get over it. It was fifteen years ago."

"I don't care how long ago it was, Travers. I don't have to do anything where you're concerned."

The way a muscle in Jack's jaw twitched told Emmy he was getting a little fed up with Joe's posturing. She could hardly blame him. Joe was acting like the adolescent he'd been when Jack had popped him.

Both men were the size of small tanks. Neither looked

ready to back down first. Not about to watch a reenactment of what had them both looking like snorting bulls, Emmy stepped between them.

Tipping up her chin, she looked up at the sandy-haired man she knew could behave much better than he was acting now. "Why did he hit you, Joe?"

"You know why he did," he muttered. "Everybody does."

"Do they?"

"Emmy." She felt Jack's hand on her shoulder, the pressure of it insistent as he tugged her back. "You don't need to do this."

"Yes, I do." Her voice was quiet, her tone utterly calm in her conviction. "What they believe about you isn't fair."

Her eyes still on Joe, feeling Jack towering protectively behind her, she moved right back between them. "Is it, Joe?"

The ex-football hero jerked his glance down to her. As if utterly certain of his response, he opened his mouth— and caught what he hadn't heard in her soft query.

There had been no uncharacteristic challenge in her voice, but he could apparently see it in her eyes as she stood her ground. In the time it took him to realize she no longer believed the story that Jack had been looking for a fight and that he'd just been in the way, the air filling Joe's impressive chest escaped in a huff.

His version wouldn't stand up very well with the other participant right there to muddy it with the truth. And the truth, if it hadn't been so long that he'd forgotten it, would hardly serve his purpose.

Male pride allowed nothing but his terse, "He knows."

She had the sudden and certain feeling that Joe knew, too, but she'd just caught sight of Charlie frowning past them all.

"You're not boilin', girl?"

Squinting through his silver-rimmed bifocals, Charlie motioned toward the sugar house. Steam from evaporating sap and smoke from a fire in the arch would rise through the cupola in a thick, billowing plume of white. Smoke from a wood fire alone looked threadier and gray.

He saw neither.

"We stopped by the Bruner place on the way over," he told her. "Tom's been chippin' ice off bucket lids all mornin', but his sap's been runnin' since noon."

Any thought of continuing to play referee vanished before she could consider why Joe's jaw was working like a grindstone. Ever since the sleet had begun falling, she had quietly feared what it seemed Charlie had just confirmed. Heavy ice broke branches. Broken branches could take out lines in the sugar bush.

Broken lines meant sap from that section couldn't reach the tank.

A broken main line meant nothing reached the tank at all.

"I have lines down."

Her uneasy conclusion met with the feel of Jack's hand at the small of her back. That small show of support drew her glance to his.

He had known what she feared. "We need to get moving," he said.

Aware of Joe watching them, she jerked her glance to where Charlie had just clipped his helmet to the side of his snowmobile. Unsnapping a leather side bag, the older man pulled out a stocking cap, yanked it over his head and reached for the snowshoes strapped across the back of the seat.

"Got us a bit of work," he concluded in his decidedly understated way.

"You're staying?" Jack asked.

Charlie gave a snort. "'Course I am. I came to sugar. Can't do that till the lines're fixed." He clamped on his snowshoes, tested the one on his left foot by bouncing on it a little. "There's sap drippin' into the snow out there."

Ignoring Joe, who'd picked up his helmet from his vehicle's seat, Jack turned toward the house. "I'm going to let Rudy out for a minute," he told her. "I'll be right back."

Even as he spoke the deputy climbed back on his snowmobile. "The phone line is down north of Doc Reid's place." Skepticism, speculation and reproach etched his craggy features. So did a hint of what looked like disbelief at her disloyalty—or, maybe, it was discomfort—before he jerked that glance away. "There are a few other people I need to go check on."

Without another word, he pulled on his helmet, started the engine with a subdued roar. Had he not just made conversation impossible, she would have told him she didn't care what he'd done as a kid. Heaven knew there wasn't a person on the planet whose judgment had been all that stellar at seventeen. It was just time to end the talk that never seemed to go away about the Larkins, and stop fueling the rumors about Jack that he'd helped fabricate. The rumors he might well have come to accept as fact himself. For a while, anyway.

She would have thanked him for coming, too. Living alone, she truly appreciated that he checked up on her the way he did everyone else. She was more concerned at the moment, though, with knowing he didn't appreciate the way she'd defended the man everyone expected her to hate.

She wasn't totally sure how she felt about that herself. She hadn't thought twice about doing what she'd done. And that wasn't like her at all.

Chapter Eight

"Ya know, Emmy. Since we won't be sugarin' tonight, I think I'd best be headin' home. It's nearin' dark and these ol' eyes don't see so good with the puny light on that snow machine."

Adding another broken branch to the growing pile, Jack saw Emmy look up from where she'd just dug away snow from a line. Her preoccupation immediately faded to chagrin.

"Oh, Charlie," she murmured, absently edging back her fleece headband with her forearm. "I didn't realize it was getting so late. Will you be okay going home?"

"'Course I will. Still got me a bit of daylight." He flipped up the collar of his insulated suit. "I'll be back after daybreak.

"You be careful."

"Always am, girl."

A rueful smile touched Emmy's mouth. "No, you're not."

Jack couldn't hear what Charlie muttered back before the old guy turned and lifted a hand in his direction.

Jack waved back, only to see Charlie frown as he brought himself to a stop, then headed toward him.

The old guy hadn't said much to him as they'd worked all afternoon. Other than to help Charlie haul a couple of the heavier branches from broken lines so he wouldn't hurt himself, they hadn't even worked together.

Beneath the man's navy stocking cap, his nose and cheeks were cherry red with cold. Nearly hidden by his mustache and beard, his mouth pressed in an upside-down *U*. His frown seemed to fill his whole face. The problem was that Jack couldn't tell if he was just thinking, if his toe was bothering him or if the man was finally about to say something he didn't want to hear about his transgressions or his father's. A scowl seemed to be pretty much his normal expression.

Hands on his hips, Charlie peered at him through the top half of his bifocals.

"Did I hear Emmy tell Joe you've come to give back that property?"

Being a little hard of hearing, it seemed he wanted to get his facts straight before heading home.

"Yeah, Charlie," he replied, wondering why he hadn't posed his question to Emmy.

"Mind if I ask why you made the trip instead of Ed?"

Because my father would never have done it, he could have said. "Because he's dead."

Charlie gave a slow, thoughtful, nod. "That condition would prevent the trip."

His mouth formed that upside-down *U* again. For a moment, anyway.

"I recall you used to work here for Emmy's dad."

It seemed he expected some sort of reply to the statement. Deciding his expression looked more thoughtful than perturbed, Jack gave him a nod of his own.

"Thought so. Explains why you knew to plug off the tap lines soon as you found a break." He lifted a gloved hand toward the broken tubing lying in the snow. "You're good help…for someone living down country."

Having said what he'd come to say, he finished with a terse little nod. Even qualified as they were, his words were high praise from a man who was probably as stingy with his compliments as he was with his smiles.

"Thanks, Charlie." Strangely relieved by what passed for the man's acceptance of his presence, Jack couldn't help smiling himself. "I'll see you in the morning."

"You bet you will," he replied, looking up the hill at all the acres they still had to cover. "Rather be workin' outside than sittin' cooped up in. Never should have let my son talk me into selling the farm and movin' in with his family," he muttered. "Man can't be happy with nothin' to do any more than he can be happy having nothin' to do but work."

Giving the collar of his insulated suit another tug to ward off the cold, he turned to snowshoe his way toward Emmy's house, where he'd left his transportation. As he did, Jack felt his own brow pinch. He had no time to wonder at the man's grumbling, though. Since the sun had dropped behind the hills, the temperature had dropped right with it.

Emmy had already returned to her task. With the pale

light fading, he needed to return to his, if for no other reason than to keep himself warm.

They had checked the ice-coated main line first and found it broken a hundred yards up the hill. While Charlie and Emmy cracked ice away and repaired that line, he had continued on up, found another break for them to fix, then started checking the maze of lines in the section leading into it.

Fallen branches had taken down some of clear lateral tubing in places. Other trees had lines that had been pulled away by the weight of the ice. The good news was that not every tree or line had been damaged. But then, Emmy probably had close to fifteen hundred trees on her land and he had barely checked a dozen.

They'd hadn't even covered half an acre. With nineteen and a half acres yet to go, he could only imagine how daunted Emmy had to feel by what lay ahead of her. The thought that she would be tackling the job with only the help of a rather disgruntled old man had him diligently moving on to the next tree. He suspected it would never occur to her to give up, though. So far she hadn't even balked. Shying from a task or responsibility simply wasn't her nature.

It apparently wasn't her nature, either, to let a challenge go undefended when she felt that challenge was wrong. Her defense of her father when he'd told her of his affair had been swift and immediate. Considering how she'd felt about her dad, he'd pretty much expected her reaction. What he hadn't expected was the way she'd stepped between him and Joe Sheldon. Literally. Even when he'd pulled her back, she stepped right in again, as determined as a mother bear protecting her cub.

He still couldn't believe she'd done that.

He glanced toward where she waded through the snow, checking each inch of the line on her way to the next tree. She'd barely taken a break since they'd started that morning. She would have to soon, though. With the light now a dusky gray, he figured they only had another ten minutes before they had to quit.

Emmy figured fifteen—though she would have worked in the sugar bush through the night, had it been possible to work in the dark. It had taken so long to repair the main line that they'd barely started checking the others.

Intent on those repairs, she'd disregarded the fact that she'd started shoveling snow at eight o'clock that morning. She hadn't allowed herself to focus on the fatigue starting to pull at her, or on how much work there was to be done. As she did with anything she had to get through, she'd focused only on doing it. One tree at a time. One line at a time.

The temperature had dropped back below freezing, turning her fingers numb inside the thin gloves she wore because it was too hard to work with the narrow tubing in thick ones. From the way Jack had zipped his parka to his throat, she knew he felt the cold, too. His undershirt and turtleneck were still draped over the chair in her kitchen, and he'd spent more time with his gloves off than on.

He'd worked even longer than she had. He'd been shoveling snow that morning even as she'd climbed out of bed.

As if he'd felt her watching him, he looked across the swath of snow separating them and nodded in the direction of the sugar house. Reluctantly she nodded back and watched him grab the rope on the sled holding their supplies to take it back with them. The wildlife had a good enough time gnawing on the lines without leaving a roll of it for them to turn into a chew toy.

The light of the bright half-moon rising over the hill relieved the encroaching darkness as they made their way through the trees to the sugar house. While Jack pulled the sled inside to store it overnight, Emmy checked the gauge on the tank with her flashlight.

Jack knew the moment he saw her expression in that pale circle of light that there wasn't enough sap to make it worth firing up the arch.

"The temperature had already started to fall before you got the main line repaired," Jack reminded her. It was also possible that there were too many breaks in the smaller lines to get sap to the main one, he thought. There just didn't seem to be any point to mentioning what she already knew and was probably already worrying about.

"Come on," he coaxed, taking her hand to lead her to the door. Personally, he wasn't the least disappointed that they didn't have to spend the next heaven-only-knew-how-long boiling and bottling syrup, then boiling water to clean everything up. He was tired. He was hungry. "Let's get to the house." With her hand in his, he felt her shiver. "You're cold."

"You must be, too. Half of your clothes are in the house."

"So, get the fire going when we get there. I'll stay outside with Rudy while he does his thing, then bring in more wood."

Emmy had given up on telling him he didn't need to help her. She had no intention of reverting at the moment, either. She hadn't realized how much it could mean to have someone anticipate what she might need, or to share chores she normally tackled on her own. Jack had been doing it all day. And all day she had been enormously grateful he was there.

Since the battery on the house generator refused to hold a charge, she needed to buy a new one. Unable to buy a new one until the roads were open, they remained at the mercy of flashlights, oil lamps, the woodstove and the living room fireplace. After stoking the woodstove and putting the chowder she'd taken from the freezer that morning on to heat, Emmy headed into the living room to start a fire in there. Between the two heat sources, the house would soon be warm enough to walk around in without shivering.

Flames had just leaped from tinder to logs when she heard Jack walk up behind her. "Rudy's food dish was empty so I filled it. He's got his nose in it and his tail's wagging."

A faint smile tugged at her mouth as she turned where she sat on the hearth. "He hates being cooped up in the house when I'm outside."

"I have the feeling he does just fine in here on his own. The stove kept the kitchen warm. He has his bed and his toys." Tugging the denim at the top of his knees, he crouched in front of her. "How about you?" he asked, searching her face in the growing firelight. "How are you doing?"

She could have said she was fine. It was what she would have said to anyone else who might have asked, because it wouldn't do any good to admit that she was feeling a tad panicked at the prospect of losing her production. But Jack already knew she was worried. She could tell by the way he watched her.

"I'm just glad it isn't worse. And it could have been," she told him, truly grateful for all that had been left un-harmed. "The ice storm of '98 lasted for days. The ice was so heavy no one could even get into their sugar bush to make repairs. The damage out there isn't nearly as bad."

Jack reached for her hands. He didn't know too many people who would have considered the state of her sugar bush and looked at what hadn't happened rather than all that had.

"Then, come on." He tugged her up, drawn by her daunt-less spirit, pushed by a need for food. "If I'm going back out there in the morning, you need to feed me. Let's eat in here. It'll be warm by the fire." Her hands felt like Popsicles in his. They felt small, too, and soft despite the cold, their bones fragile beneath the brush of his thumb over her wrist.

The feel of her skin against his reminded him of a hunger of a different sort. As tired and vulnerable as she looked, as easily as she allowed his touch, it would be so easy to draw her hands around his neck—and pick up where they'd left off that morning in the hallway.

Since his reasons for letting her go that morning hadn't changed, he ignored the stirring in his body and reluc-tantly let her go again. Wanting a distraction, he picked up the brass hurricane lamps she'd left on the coffee table and headed for the fireplace to light their candles. "You can tell me about Charlie."

As if conscious of his thoughts, or maybe remember-ing those moments in the hall herself, she quickly turned to clear the rest of the table. "What about him?"

"He mentioned something about having let his son talk him into selling his maple farm." He had also mentioned that a man wasn't any happier with too much time on his hands than he was having no time at all. Jack figured he fit pretty well into that last category himself. He'd just never thought of himself as that unhappy. Certainly not as unhappy as Charlie seemed to be. "Why did he do that?"

Emmy put everything from the table back on the unfinished mantel, telling him as she did that Charlie had done it because he hadn't thought he'd had any other choice at the time. On the way into the kitchen to put bread in foil and heat it on the woodstove, she explained that Charlie had needed a hip replaced a few years ago but had balked at the surgery.

It got to where keeping up the fifty acres of land became too much for him with a bad hip, she confided, heating milk for cocoa. Since his son, Mark, who taught and coached at the high school couldn't help him, Mark and Mark's wife had talked the Moorehouses into selling the farm and moving in with them because they were closer to the center of the community. The Moorehouses sold the operation and their home to the oldest Bruner boy who'd recently married and wanted a big sugaring operation of his own. The one his carpenter father ran was more of a hobby farm and nowhere near large enough to support a family.

"So what happened?" Jack asked as she dished up their bowls of chowder and they carried them and the rest of their supper back to the warmth of the blazing fire. "I noticed a little limp, but he gets around like a man half his age."

Watching him absently scratch Rudy's ear when her dog curled up under the table, Emmy sat down on the sofa beside him and handed him the bread she'd wrapped in a plaid cloth napkin.

"The limp is from his gout. The bad hip was on the other side. He finally had it replaced after he fell off a ladder because it gave out on him."

"What was he doing on a ladder?"

"Picking apples," she replied, sounding as if that were simply Charlie. "He didn't break anything, but he could have. He said Mrs. Moorehouse made him so miserable telling him how miserable he was going to be if he couldn't get around at all that he finally gave in and had the operation. He says now he wishes he'd done it ten years ago. Then he'd still have his farm."

Her mug sat on the table in front of her. As she reached for it, Jack studied the lines of her pretty profile. She was easy to look at, easy to listen to. When the past wasn't interfering, he was also finding her easy to be with.

"Why didn't he do it sooner?"

The golden light of the fire seemed to catch in her hair when she glanced toward him. "You should know that. You lived here." She spoke the reminder as he leaned forward to spoon up a steaming chunk of potato. "There are still a lot of people around who don't trust anything they haven't lived with pretty near all their lives. Especially the older ones. To them, modern is 'newfangled,' and anything like that takes a long time to get used to. It took him a decade to get used to the idea of walking around with a bionic body part."

"You've lived here all your life, but you're not that way." Between bites of the warm and welcome meal, Jack considered her reliance on her computers and the updated sugaring equipment she would buy when she could afford it. "You don't sound much like the other locals who were born here, either."

He knew for a fact that he'd never heard her use *new-fangled* before, and she'd didn't tend to drop her *g*s from her *ing*s the way many of the older folk around there did.

He'd actually worked hard on that one himself. Nothing set a person apart to a flatlander like the dialect and colloquialisms of the rural country. As important as it was to preserve those regionalisms, it had taken him only a few weeks after they'd left Maple Mountain to realize that in college and in business, he would get farther faster if he sounded like the talking heads on network television news.

He wondered if that was who she'd studied, too.

"I don't mind if visitors think Maple Mountain or my B and B is quaint," she admitted, dipping into chowder herself. "I even play up that aspect for business. I just don't want the people I do business with to think I am.

"Here," she said, handing him more bread since his was already gone.

Absently thanking her as he took it, he slid her a sideways glance, told her that *quaint* wasn't a word he would ever use to describe her, and turned back to his supper.

Curious about the absolute certainty in his voice, she wanted to know how he *would* describe her, then canceled the thought when she considered his basis for comparison. Doing what he did for a living, the women he worked and socialized with were undoubtedly smart, savvy and far more sophisticated than she could ever hope to be. Sitting in the middle of her "quaint" little house, looking like something the cat had dragged in and grown bored with, she decided there were some things she was probably better off not knowing. At least not just then.

She focused instead on the fact that Jack's bowl was almost empty. The sandwich she'd hurriedly thrown together for him for lunch had probably worn off hours ago.

She brought him more chowder, poured more cocoa. He had worked hard. They all had. But Jack had been the one to move the heaviest branches, the one to clear away the deepest snow, the one who'd pitched in as if there had never been any question about whether or not he would help.

He needed a stocking cap, she thought as she returned to her supper, thinking of how chilly it would be in the morning. She'd already asked Charlie if Jack could borrow a pair of snow pants to help insulate him from the morning and evening cold, but she should have Jack leave his jeans and socks outside his door tonight so she could wash them and leave them by the woodstove to dry overnight.

It was the least she could do. Except, possibly, to tell him how much she appreciated his help.

With her hands wrapped around her mug, she murmured, "Thank you, Jack."

He leaned back from his now empty bowl. "For what?"

"For all you did today. I don't know what Charlie and I would have done without your help."

He lifted one shoulder in a shrug, reached for his own mug. "Less."

"I mean it," she murmured, unwilling to let him minimize his contribution. "I'd still be out there shoveling snow from the sugar house and hauling in wood if it hadn't been for you. We wouldn't have made it into the sugar bush at all."

"You'd have checked the sugar bush when Charlie got here."

"I need to be ready to boil when the tank fills. It wouldn't do any good to repair lines and have the tank fill if I can't get in to boil it."

"So, it's a chicken-or-egg thing? What…?" he asked, when she looked at him as if he'd just turned as dense as the sugar bush in September.

"I'm trying to thank you," she explained, not sure he'd caught that. "I'm glad you're here, Jack. I really appreciate all you did today."

She was glad he was there.

At her quiet admission, Jack skimmed back a strand of hair that had long ago loosened itself from the piece of gathered green fabric holding her windblown ponytail. She allowed his touch as easily as she had when he'd taken her hands before. She would allow his kiss, too, he thought, trailing his finger along her jaw. He could see it in her eyes when they met his once more.

"I'm glad I'm here, too," he told her, and avoided the temptation of her lovely mouth the only way he could think of without leaving the room.

Setting down both their mugs, he took her by the shoulders as he leaned back against the corner of the sofa. Coaxing her toward him, he tucked her back to his chest and folded his arms around her. He was glad he was there, he thought, liking the way she relaxed against him. He had actually enjoyed the mind-clearing physical labor the day had brought, too. It had given him something productive to do after the local law enforcement had jerked around with his blood pressure. "So, you're welcome. And thank you, too."

Her voice sounded as quiet as the crackle of the fire gleaming off the table's dark, shining wood. "For what?"

He focused on the comfort of that fire, the warmth that had taken the chill from the room, his bones, and the feel of her resting so trustingly against him. Even thinking about how well her slender little body fit his seemed safer than thinking too much about what she'd done. He didn't want it to matter as much as it did. "For what you said to Joe."

"Oh," she murmured, and apparently decided to let it go at that.

He thought about asking why she'd done it, but he had the feeling she didn't want to look too closely at her obvious defense of him. He just hoped that what she'd done wouldn't cause her any trouble.

Not sure how he'd straighten the situation out if it did, thinking he'd worry about that later, he murmured, "Say 'you're welcome.'"

A small smile slipped into her voice. "You're welcome," she murmured.

The temptation to kiss her grew stronger. The thought that she had come so willingly into his arms made it grow stronger still. But his sense of fair play battled the desire stirring in his blood. If he kissed her, he wouldn't want to stop, and he wasn't prepared to deal with any more uncomfortable feelings where she was concerned.

The guilt he'd carried about her before had been because of his father's actions. If she was hurt now, it would be his fault. He would leave Maple Mountain as soon as the roads were passable, and the last thing he wanted to do was take advantage of her. She'd been through enough because of a Travers without having her think he'd used her somehow.

He slipped a little lower on the sofa, tightened his arms a little more around her. "Comfortable?" he asked.

Her quiet "Very" sounded almost like a sigh.

"Good," he murmured, and contented himself to do nothing other than hold her. It was what she had seemed to need that morning, anyway, before her scent and her softness had hooked him and she'd played utter havoc with his libido. With the quiet surrounding them, the fatigue of the day seeping into his bones, just holding her for her sake didn't seem like such a difficult thing to do.

Emmy had thermoses of coffee and cocoa filled and tuna sandwiches packed in the backpack when Charlie arrived an hour after the sun rose the next morning.

She had been up earlier than usual, anxious to get started on the long day ahead. Anticipation at the thought of being with Jack had prodded her, too. She'd almost fallen asleep in his arms last night. She probably would have, had he not finally tugged her to her feet, helped her with the dishes, then taken her by the shoulders and aimed her for her bedroom.

He had freely offered the comfort of his arms. Yet, he had made no attempt at all to repeat what had happened in the hallway. With everything else on her mind that morning, she wouldn't let herself question what was going on with him, any more than she would allow herself to question why she had so easily allowed his touch. She simply accepted it as the gift it seemed to be, and tried hard to tell herself that what she felt most toward him was simply gratitude for his help.

"Got it," he said, grabbing the backpack when she reached for it and headed out the mudroom door with his snowshoes in his other hand.

Giving Rudy instructions to be a good boy, along with an extra treat because he'd have to stay in alone again today, she grabbed her own gear and a black knit cap for Jack to wear. Heading out behind him, she saw Charlie hand him warm gloves and a pair of navy waterproof pants to pull on over his jeans.

Jack smiled at the unexpected thoughtfulness. "Hey, Charlie, thanks."

Charlie's only reply was a typically gruff, "Emmy said you needed 'em" before he said, "Mornin'," to her and they headed for the woods.

"Before I forget," Charlie said, as if forgetting were a distinct possibility at his age, "Joe came by on his way to west county. He didn't get a chance to check on folk there yesterday, and comin' here wasn't on his way.

"Anyways, Jack," he continued, rubbing his nose with the back of his glove, "he wanted me to tell you that Joanna over at the post office is a notary. He heard you're lookin' for one. Said, too, to tell you that if you're needin' a phone, the one at the general store is still workin'. He thought you might have business that needs takin' care of, bein' the plows won't get the road to the highway open till tomorrow or day after."

Jack glanced to where the older man followed him a few steps back. Charlie had almost said more in the last minute than he had all of yesterday afternoon.

If Charlie found anything unusual about Joe's message it wasn't evident in his wizened features. Emmy seemed to catch some significance to it, though. Her glance had darted to his, then away, as if what she'd just heard wasn't necessarily good news.

Jack wasn't quite sure how to take it, either. His inquiries at the motel and the store about a notary had obviously made their way to Joe. Since the guy knew he wanted to give the property back, he'd obviously figured out that the transferring document needed to be notarized. Jack could understand that Joe would want to help him convey the property to Emmy for her sake, but for Joe to have considered his business concerns and send word of a working phone made it almost seem as if he were offering some sort of truce.

From the moment his old teammate had first resurrected the bitterness between them, Jack hadn't thought it possible to put the old grudge to rest. For either of them. With that small capitulation on Joe's part, thanks to Emmy, it didn't seem so hopeless after all.

"Thanks, Charlie," he finally said, and dropped back to walk with the woman studiously avoiding his eyes.

He figured Charlie's mention of the notary had her thinking he would start pushing her again about the property. He wasn't about to mention it now, though. She had too much else to deal with. So did he.

"Mind if I borrow your snowmobile?"

"The key's in the ignition."

"Thanks. I'm going to go use the phone at the store. I shouldn't be gone long." He fell back a step, his glance now on her back. "What do you want me to pick up while I'm there?"

"Bread. And milk," she called back, and tried very hard not to think about what Charlie had said about the road to the highway being open tomorrow.

Jack had no idea how a plow could clear the road all the way from the highway, through Maple Mountain and out to Emmy's house by morning—unless all the major roads in the county had been cleared yesterday and the plows were now being sent to less populated places. He remembered from having grown up here that it had sometimes been days before a plow came through after a big storm.

Wondering if he could find out how far away the plow was for certain, he tramped through the snow and up the general store's shoveled steps. He was knocking snow from his boots when the squeaky screen door opened. Grabbing it, he held it for a pretty young woman he didn't recognize, but who smiled at him anyway.

"Say hi to Dr. Reid for me, Jenny," came Agnes's hollered request from inside. "And you be careful out there in the snow. You don't need to be fallin' in your condition!"

"He says hi back. And I'll be careful," called the woman who barely looked pregnant at all in her short ski jacket. Carrying a bag of groceries, she carefully made her way between the berms of snow lining the path that had been shoveled the length of Main.

Jack was watching her go, and wondering at the mini population boom in Maple Mountain, since Joe's wife apparently was pregnant, too, when he heard Agnes holler again.

"I'm not heating the great outdoors. Come on in and close the door before it's warmer out there than it is in here."

The admonishment had a friendly edge to it. One that Jack had a feeling would fade as soon as Agnes saw who it was letting out the heat blazing from the old pot-bellied stove.

Remembering his last reception there made his smile feel a little strained.

"Good morning, Mrs. Waters."

Agnes stood on the far side of the counter, stacking boxed candles on its scratched surface. Two other women stood back by the dairy case. The electricity was on here, he noticed, but Agnes had obviously had a run on candles and lamp oil from those who weren't so fortunate. Only three bottles of oil remained in the nearly empty box beside her.

What he noticed most was the way Agnes's smile faltered.

"Mornin', Jack," she allowed, though what he saw wasn't the disapproval she'd treated him with before. As she brought a little of that smile back, her rounded features held something that looked more like curiosity, along with a hint of embarrassment. "Joe said you might be stoppin' by."

So that was the reason for the attitude shift, he thought. Joe had passed on his purpose for being there. The woman with the birds appliquéd to her sweatshirt, quail this time, knew he wasn't building condos after all.

"I understand your phone works."

"It does."

"Mind if I use it? I'll put everything on my calling card."

The women by the dairy case, one in a purple stocking cap who looked vaguely familiar, the other in pink who looked as if she might be her daughter, already had their heads together. They whispered as they watched him, then hurriedly looked away when they realized he'd noticed them talking.

"That'd be just fine," Agnes replied. "That phone line north of town seems to be the first to go down whenever we get ice. Don't know what the problem is," she continued, sounding strangely friendly as she motioned him to follow her. "What I do know is that the phone company won't be here to fix it till the road gets plowed."

"Any idea when that will be?"

"I hear from Joe that the plow's due in here tonight. The driver stays over at the motel, then heads up north from here."

She led him along the wall of ice fishing gear to the back of the store and through a door that opened into her stockroom. "You'll have more privacy if you use the phone in here," she confided, flipping on the light to indicate a small desk littered with invoices. "People keep comin' and goin' out front."

Even as she spoke, the bell over the door gave its cheery little tinkle.

"Thanks," he murmured as she turned away. "And when you see Joe thank him, too."

"I'll do that," she assured him, and headed off to see who'd just come in.

The women out front were already talking when he closed the door on the low drone of chatter and picked up the phone.

He called his new office first to get an update on the situation there, only to learn that the edge of the storm had moved as far south as Boston and that the New York office had actually closed early yesterday afternoon. Since he hadn't been the only one to suffer because of weather, it was much easier to reschedule everything for the following week, which would leave him with the schedule from hell, but he was accustomed to that.

He then called his old landlady to make sure his possessions had been packed and shipped, only to learn that the weather had delayed that, too. The movers were now due to arrive today. That information necessitated a call back to his new assistant to coordinate the details with the moving company and his new landlord.

Because he was anxious to get back to the sugar bush, not bothering to question why, he made the call to his mom as short as possible.

"I'm fine, Mom," he assured her, when Ruth Travers asked the first thing she always did when she heard his voice. "I'm still in Maple Mountain. I'll give you the details later about the Larkins," he promised, certain his location alone had raised a dozen questions. "There's just something I need to know. Who was it Stan was involved with?"

Aware that he might be heard by anyone on the other side of the door, Jack stayed away from it and kept his voice low. It just never occurred to him as his mom told him everything she could recall, that Agnes had picked up the phone by the cash register to see if he was still on the line— and that she was now listening to everything they said.

Chapter Nine

Wildfire didn't spread as fast as gossip in Maple Mountain. Even with only half the telephones in the area working, news that the Traverses claimed Stan Larkins had cheated on his wife and had an illegitimate child made it through the core of the community and out to Emmy's place by midafternoon.

That was when Charlie's wife, Mary, arrived on her son's snowmobile, and gave the two sets of three short horn blasts that was their signal when Charlie and Emmy were working in the sugar bush.

Hearing the distant beeps, Emmy left the men where they were running a new line and headed down to meet her. Charlie had told her earlier that Mary planned to bring over a casserole for Emmy and Jack's supper. The dear lady often sent meals for her and Charlie when the two of them were up late sugaring. Mary also usually left whatever it was she brought in the mudroom or brought it to the sugar house. The fact that she'd used their signal meant she wanted something other than to simply drop off the much-appreciated meal.

With a smile for her nearest neighbor, Emmy emerged from the woods and waved at the woman in bright blue wading through the snow toward her. The curls around the edges of her cap were as white as the ground, her cheeks pink from her ride over on the snowmobile she drove with the abandon of a teenager.

Natives of the north country tended to be of hearty, headstrong stock.

"Afternoon, dear," she said, motioning toward the house. "I set a cooler with a casserole and an apple crumb cake inside your mudroom. Closed the door to the kitchen," she added, "so Rudy wouldn't get to sniffin' around and try to help himself to chicken and vegetables."

"Crumb cake, too?" Emmy's smile grew. "Thank you, Mary."

Raising a mittened hand, she waved off the thanks as if her generosity were nothing. "You know you're more than welcome. Cake dips a bit in the center, but I think it'll taste okay. Can't get that old wood oven of my son's to keep a steady temperature the way you can an electric range. But their generator only runs the fridge and the furnace, so what can you do?"

"I'm sure it'll be wonderful."

The compliment should have met with a smile. And it did. In a way. It was just that the usual brightness was missing from it. That brightness had also faded from her keen hazel eyes.

"I had to go to Waters's store for brown sugar for the cake," she prefaced. "Heard somethin' there you might be needin' to know. Leastwise before you hear it from someone else."

The quick caution in the woman's expression blended with a heavy hint of apology. That same apology seemed to shadow her tone.

"Agnes told me and Claire that Jack Travers came in this morning to use the phone. She had him use the one in the storeroom to give him privacy, and picked up the other one after a while to see if he was still on it.

"Seems he was," she concluded. "Agnes says she heard him talkin' to his mom about your dad having been…indiscreet," she decided to call it, since she wasn't the sort to sensationalize details herself. "She seemed to think you knew what he was sayin' because he mentioned to his mom that you'd had questions."

Even as Mary spoke, Emmy felt her heart sink. If Agnes had told Mary and Claire McGraw, who happened to be *the* biggest gossip around, then she had shared what she'd overheard with everyone who'd walked into the store.

Mary's concerned deepened. "You did know he was sayin' it, didn't you, Emmy?"

Pushing back the hair the breeze blew past the headband covering her ears, Emmy nodded. "I'd asked him to get more information from his mom," she allowed. Her tone fell. "The grapevine has to be on overload by now."

"I'd imagine."

At the woman's rueful comment, Emmy blew a long low breath.

"Thank you, Mary," she said, because she truly did appreciate what the woman had just done. Charlie's wife wasn't asking questions herself. She wasn't judging, offering her opinion or hinting around to find out how Emmy felt about her father supposedly having another child, or how she felt about Jack and his mother for believing such a thing. The kindly woman who'd once told her how much it meant to her to have her husband doing something he loved, had simply come to warn her—and give her time to react to the news before she found herself confronted by less-sensitive souls.

As it was, Emmy had about fifteen seconds before a high-pitched "Oh, Emmy!" pierced the lovely afternoon quiet.

Realizing who it was chugging up her driveway, it was all she could do not to close her eyes and groan. Bertie Buell, the fog of her breath puffing like a locomotive and bearing down with about as much speed, plowed toward them on snowshoes and swinging ski poles to make her rangy frame move as fast as it could go.

"I'm glad you're out here," she called as she drew closer, then stopped to pull the cap off her flyaway salt-and-pepper hair now that she'd worked herself into a sweat. Making a two-mile trek from town wasn't extraordinary for Bertie. It was something the lean, leathery woman might have done just for the exercise on any other day. Today, however, it appeared that an invigorating workout was the last thing on her narrow little mind. "Didn't want to have to holler all over the woods lookin' for him."

She finally glanced to the woman she served with on the community women's league and church board. "Afternoon, Mary."

"Bertie," Mary said, and looked back to Emmy as if to apologize for not having given her more lead time.

"Him?" Emmy asked.

"That Travers boy. Where is he?"

Not at all sure what the woman's problem was, Emmy motioned vaguely behind her. "He's working in the sugar bush with Charlie."

"Well, I imagine you can't get rid of him soon enough. But I got a thing or two I need to say to him before you do. I can see where you'd want to wait until you get your papers signed on that property before you run him off, and I'm glad you're making him work off his room and board, but I don't know how you can be civil to him starting such rumors. If he was trying to clear his father's name by giving back that land, he did a lousy job of it. Slandering a man is even worse than stealing his land."

Bertie practically vibrated with indignation. But then, being indignant was pretty much the prudish and opinionated woman's natural state. She wasn't happy unless she was in a huff, and she could get herself in a huff over just about anything. The problem was that she saw everything as either black or white—and wouldn't recognize a shade of gray if she painted her house with it.

The bigger problem was that she appeared to see herself as Emmy's champion. She also had far less information than Emmy did and none of the reluctant perspectives Emmy had forced herself to realize.

"Jack didn't come back here to start rumors, Bertie. And it's only slander if it's not true."

Incredulity washed the woman's thin face. "You're not saying you believe him, are you?"

"I don't believe he's making this up as he goes, if that's what you mean. His mother, either," she said, thinking of how Ruth Travers had sent her apologies back with Jack for not having more information to give her. All she'd recalled was that the woman had been a young widow over in West Pond, and that she had apparently moved to Montpelier sometime before the child was born.

It seemed from what Emmy remembered seeing in the ledgers that her dad had several jobs in the area around the little community thirty miles away. As she'd thought more about it it seemed as if he'd stopped taking jobs there after a while, too.

She needed to look through the ledgers again. In the meantime she needed to deal with the woman looking at her as if she'd just turned traitor and betrayed them all.

"Why, Emmy Larkin. I never thought I'd see the day that you'd defend a Travers. And against your own father's reputation."

"I'm not choosing one over the other," she insisted, refusing to let the woman put her in such a position. "My father was a good man." And he did his best to protect me, she thought, remembering how Jack had made sure she saw that. "So is Jack."

"Giving somebody back what's theirs doesn't make a man good. It's what a person's supposed to do. And don't forget what he did to Joe," she reminded her, clearly prepared to set her on the straight and narrow. "A good man doesn't go getting himself into fights the way he did."

The sad thing about Bertie, Emmy thought, was that the woman thought she was right. But the middle-aged spinster, whose life seemed to revolve around everyone else's, hadn't a clue what she was talking about. Emmy knew the sort of man Jack was. She also knew that some minds were impossible to change and that Bertie Buell's was set in concrete.

"It was one fight," she countered flatly. "And you might want to ask Joe just what it was that happened." She doubted Joe would ever admit exactly what had happened in the locker room that day. She suspected he'd claim he couldn't remember. Or wave it off as no longer of consequence. But she doubted he'd continue claiming Jack had been the bad guy.

Bertie opened her mouth, clearly intent on recalling other transgressions. Looking as if she were sure there were more, just unable to recall them at the moment, she let out a huff.

Temporarily thwarted, she switched victims. "What about this other woman, then?"

Other woman? she thought, only to realize she was talking about her dad.

For years Emmy had bitten her tongue, said nothing about how intrusive she found some people and the meddling that somehow passed for concern. But Jack had come to Maple Mountain to set things right. He'd faced hostility because of it, yet that hadn't prevented him from coming back the day after he'd first arrived to see that he accomplished his goal. Taking a risk to right this particular wrong was exactly what she needed to do, too.

"You know, Bertie. None of this is anyone's business but mine." Certainly, it was none of hers. "My father has been dead for years. Let him rest. As for Jack and his father, people have seen them as fair game for so long that folks believe anything anyone says about them…as long as it's not something good. It's time to let them rest, too."

Crossing her arms over the nerves jumping in her stomach, she added a quiet, "Please."

Letting it all go wasn't going to happen. Even as the woman pursed her lips and pulled on her hat, Emmy knew speculation would run rampant about her father's purported affair, her parent's relationship and her defection to the side of the apparent enemy.

With all her purposes for making the trip from town frustrated, the woman took off in the direction she'd come.

"I know you hate talk, Emmy. But you can't stop it."

She glanced to the woman who'd just reached over to pat her arm.

"Look at it this way," Mary suggested, her smile deepening the lines of wisdom in her face. "People will speculate, but they're usually kinder to the dead than the living. The other thing is that while they're talkin' about your papa, they're leavin' someone else alone."

Emmy smiled at that last one. "Mom used to say that."

"You should remember it, then."

The smile faltered. "Mary," Emmy began. "Did you ever hear of my father having an affair?"

"I can't say that I did. But that's not the sort of thing that's likely to get around unless someone saw him, or he or your mama talked about it to other folk who talked about it in turn."

"Do you think it's possible?"

"Wouldn't care to speculate." She gave her arm one last pat. "But I will tell you that if you see reason to forgive what went on between your family and the Traverses, then

I'm of a mind to let go of my ill thinkin' about 'em, too. Especially that young man helpin' you out there," she added, nodding toward the woods before she pushed up the sleeve of her parka to check her watch as if she should be going soon. From the basket strapped behind the snowmobile seat, it appeared she'd made supper for someone else, too. The Hanleys, Emmy would bet, since they'd be in the same straights she was in. "Charlie said this morning that he needed to help him clear the snow off his car since the road should be open in the mornin', but I think he's going to hate to see him go."

Mary's reminder that Jack would soon leave managed to overshadow every other thought as Emmy returned to where the men worked in the lengthening afternoon shadows. Jack and Charlie had their heads together over a line they were splicing when Jack glanced toward her.

Telling Charlie he'd be right back, he left the older man fixing a new hanger to a tree trunk and snowshoed his way to where she'd gone back to checking a line for splits and leaks.

She must not have done a very good job of masking her disquiet. She could practically feel his frown on the top of her head.

"What's wrong?"

I'm not ready for you to leave, she thought. "Agnes overheard you on the phone with your mom," she said instead, since that had added a knot to her stomach, too.

Swift as a slash, Jack quietly swore. "Oh, man," he muttered a moment later. "I'm sorry, Emmy. I know I wasn't talking that loud."

"Agnes was eavesdropping on another phone. But you know what?" she asked, keeping her focus on her task as she slowly moved along the line. "It doesn't matter. Now that word is out, the damage to his reputation is done. So there's no reason to hide the rest of it."

A hint of skepticism entered his voice. "What do you mean?"

"I told Mary what you told me," she said, feeling oddly calm. "About how that was why your dad called the loan, and how they kept that reason to themselves. And about how it seemed people didn't give any consideration to him having a family of his own to support. I don't think he was fair," she qualified to him, because her dad had been cheated out of the value of the land, "but, if it all is true, your parents protected mine when they could have at least partially defended themselves. If people are going to talk, they might as well have both sides of the story."

"Hey, Jack! Can you give me a hand here?"

Jack's tall shadow remained still next to hers. It seemed there was something he wanted to say. It also seemed he figured that now wasn't the time to say it.

"I better go see what he needs."

"I think he just wants your company," she murmured, and would have given him a smile had she not just found another leak.

Emmy waited all afternoon for Jack to bring up his departure. As anxious as he had to be to get out of there, she knew it had to be on his mind. Yet as they worked their way through the trees, he said nothing about it. He said nothing, either, after Charlie left at dusk, or after they fired up the arch and the little generator at the sugar house for lights so they could boil what little sap there was in the tank because she hated to see it go to waste.

It wasn't until he said that Charlie had mentioned a neighbor's boy who cleared driveways that she thought he might tell her he would leave as soon as the plow came through. But his only comment was that he wanted to hire him to use his snow blower on Emmy's driveway and to dig out his car.

"Charlie said the kid lives not far from his son's house. He'll go over in the morning on his way here to ask him to come out. You don't have to pay him for it. I will," he insisted, because he seemed to know she was about to protest the extravagance. "It makes more sense for us to spend our time in the sugar bush. If we don't run into any nasty surprises, we should be able to finish up that northwest quarter by tomorrow night."

It took a moment for what he'd just said to fully register. But she'd barely realized he didn't intend to leave tomorrow after all, when the sudden seriousness in his eyes stalled her smile.

"And, Emmy," he said, sounding as tired as she felt as he watched her warm her hands in the heat radiating from beneath the huge pan. "Thank you for what you did today."

Beside them steam rose from the evaporator, filling the air with warm moisture and the sweet, familiar scent of the sap. Watching him look from the wisps and tendrils billowing above the pan's metal sides, she didn't have to ask to know what had him looking so grave. She knew. She had all but defended his father by letting it be known she held him responsible for nothing beyond selling the land.

"I just want to set things right," she replied, because she knew he couldn't do it alone. "And, Jack," she continued, much as he had when he'd said her name moments ago. "I have the feeling from what you've said about your father that your relationship with him was…difficult," she allowed, truly sorry he hadn't known the closeness she'd shared with hers. "But I'm sorry you lost him."

Jack suddenly seemed at a loss for words. He simply stood there, faint lines forming in his brow as his eyes searched hers—until he slowly lifted his hand to her face.

He touched his knuckles to her cheek, something raw shifting through his eyes. "Thank you." He murmured the words as the lines in his brow deepened, but even then his expression grew shuttered and he inched his hand from her skin.

She couldn't believe how disappointed she felt at that loss of contact. Hoping to mask the feeling, she gave him a small smile and moved away to unpack empty containers before the sap turned to syrup and they had to start the process of packaging it up.

Jack watched her go, thought seriously about going after her. He just wasn't sure what he'd do when he reached her, so he stayed where he was and asked if she wanted him to check at the store for a battery for her house generator in the morning.

She told him that the Waters's store didn't stock the kind she needed. She'd have to drive to St. Johnsbury when the roads were open or order one from a catalog and the UPS man could bring it. They did a lot of shopping by catalog in Maple Mountain.

He remembered that. And remembering it led to conversation that finally allowed the mental distance he knew he needed.

Emmy had an absolute gift for throwing curves. Her defense of him yesterday had been surprising enough. That she had explained why his father had done what he had was something he never would have expected at all. But when she'd told him she was sorry his father had died, that had meant far more to him than he could have imagined.

The fact that it did mean so much was what had made him pull back from her, and what made him keep his hands to himself as they went about the work of the evening. That deep and dangerous feeling was what kept him from pulling her into his arms a few hours later when they made their way into the house for the wonderful meal Charlie's wife had brought, and later still when she looked at him with a tired smile at the foot of the stairs and told him to rest well. It helped him avoid that same temptation in the morning when she bumped the heel of her hand to her forehead as he walked into the kitchen and told him she'd been so tired last night that she'd forgotten to wash his jeans. She would do them tonight, for sure.

"You have enough to do without taking care of my laundry," he told her, and headed for the coffee before he could kiss the quick frown from her forehead.

The act of not touching her soon seemed to claim every moment when she was near. He had no idea how not doing something could require so much concentration or energy, but he figured it must be something like not smoking when a person is trying to quit. A person was so conscious of what he wanted that not having it claimed front and center in his mind.

Front and center in Emmy's thoughts was the fact that Jack truly seemed in no hurry to leave. Even when Charlie arrived after breakfast and said he'd seen the plow about a mile down the road, which meant the road from Maple Mountain to the highway was already open, Jack's only interest seemed to be in getting into the sugar bush.

She was afraid to trust why he was staying. It didn't make any sense to her at all. But she was too grateful for his help and his solid presence to question it. She was afraid to trust her growing feelings for him, too, as they set off through the snow once more.

She'd told herself that the pull she felt toward him didn't matter. She knew how Jack felt about his work. She knew how he felt about living in the city. She knew the stillness surrounding them as they crunched their way through the woods would eventually drive him nuts. He'd said so himself. She also knew that he'd worked hard to get where he was and that the excitement and lure of his work was as seductive to him as the need for stability was to her.

She was a practical woman. Always had been. Always would be. Therefore, it made no sense at all to start falling in love with him, much less to start imagining what her life could be like with him in it.

The problem was that, practical or not, she was already a little in love with him. Maybe a lot, for all she knew. She'd never really been in love before. And she already knew how good it was being with him. It seemed she could talk to him about nearly anything. She could share. And he shared back.

She liked the way he told her as they worked that morn-

ing about the resort his company was building on Hilton
Head and how animated he became describing its fountains
and lounges and sweeping grounds. She liked the way he
asked what she thought the most important features of a
room were for guests, since she was in the business, as he
put it, and that her opinions truly seemed to matter to him.
Mostly she liked the concern he showed for Charlie and
how hard it seemed to be on the older man and his wife
living with their son and his family.

What she didn't care for was the void that threatened inside her when the thought of his leaving returned. Or
maybe what she felt was simply overwhelmed when she
reached the rise of the hill they'd worked their way up late
that afternoon and saw the deep drifts of snow and broken
branches on the north-facing slope on the other side.

Dusk was already settling around them. Charlie had left
a few minutes ago and somewhere down slope, Jack was
splicing a new line into the main one.

She couldn't even see some of the lines ahead of her.
The wind had driven the deep snow up the trunks, piling
it over the spiles. The only way to see if lines were down
would be to dig them out.

Soon, it would only be her and Charlie, and she was
looking at far more work than the two of them could rea-
sonably handle before sugaring season was over. But she
couldn't let herself think in such terms. She had no choice
but to do what she always did and keep moving forward
because to stop meant she had no chance of recovering her
production at all. And that meant she had no business
standing there wasting time.

Not allowing herself to think beyond that thought, hating the sense of panic finally making itself felt, she stepped into snow that buried her snowshoes, and started digging the deep and heavy stuff from the nearest tree.

Chapter Ten

Dusk was rapidly settling into darkness when Emmy heard Jack call her name over the rise.

The temperature had taken a nosedive with the sunset. It didn't help matters that the wind that had gusted off and on all afternoon had grown steadier in the past few minutes. Although she was accustomed to cold, she could feel it working its way through her clothes, stiffening her fingers, sucking heat from her muscles. Her ears were even starting to ache from the freezing air penetrating her fleece headband. Still, given a choice between heat and light right then, she'd have taken light in a heartbeat.

She could no longer see the clear tubing against the snow. The entire downslope was covered in deep-blue shadows.

Here, where the sun reached for only a few hours a day,

the ice hadn't completely melted from the trees as it had where sun had bathed other exposures since the storm. As everywhere else, the snow had become heavier with the thaw and freeze of the days. It was just deeper, harder to move through, harder to clear away.

Stepping through the crust that had frozen over it again, she started to call back to Jack, only to see his silhouette clear the rise twenty feet above her.

Now that he knew where she was, she went right back to her task. She moved quickly, as quickly as she could considering the deepening cold and the snow bogging her down. She just wanted to get to the next tree. And maybe the one next to that.

"Emmy," he called again, his voice carrying on the frigid breeze. "There's no sense starting another section now. It's going to be dark in a couple of minutes."

Jack didn't know how she could see as it was. He couldn't even tell what she was doing as she knelt in the deep drift of snow. There was no mistaking her intention to keep doing it, though. Even with her slender shape little more than a shadow against the pearl-like brightness of the snow, it was impossible to miss her resolve.

He stepped over a fallen icy branch and lifted another out of the way. Finally close enough to see the trench she was digging with her hands, he realized it wasn't just her quiet, incredible stubbornness pushing her. What he saw seemed more like a desperate determination that refused to acknowledge just how impossible the task surrounding her appeared to be.

Even in the dim and shadowy twilight, he could see branches down everywhere.

"Hey, Emmy. Come on," he coaxed, reaching her side. "You can't even see out here."

"I don't need to see to feel where the line is."

So that's what she was doing, he thought, watching her edge away from him. He couldn't see the line himself. Neither could she. But by holding on to what she'd exposed, she could feel where to dig snow away from it.

It seemed that the desperate part of her determination was getting the better of her. She crawled back, still on her knees, digging with her hands. Even wearing gloves, he knew her hands had to be freezing. The rest of her had to feel like an icicle, too. He did, and he had on his jacket.

She'd left hers on the sled. Having noticed it, he'd brought it with him.

He held it out to her. "At least put this on."

"When I get to the next tree. I don't want to lose the line."

"I'll help you find it."

The distant howl of a wolf creased her brow as she finally straightened. As if remembering that Rudy was in the house, safe from anything on the hunt, she dismissed the lonely sound and absently reached for her parka.

Bumping her hand against his as she took it, she winced.

"What's the matter?"

"My hands are just cold."

"Emmy." Trying for patience, he tugged off her gloves for her so she wouldn't get the snow stuck to them inside her jacket sleeves. "Tell me you wouldn't be doing this if I wasn't here."

"Doing what?"

"Working in the dark."

She barely glanced at him as, shivering, she struggled

into the insulated outerwear and reached for her gloves. "The moon will be up soon."

Her fingers were too stiff to fasten her parka's closures. Leaving it open, she worked her gloves back on, lowering her head so he couldn't see how difficult the simple task was and prepared to get back to work. If she could just clear to the next tree, it would be one less she'd have to do tomorrow.

Catching her arm before she could turn around, his tone went as flat as ice on a pond. "You know something?" he muttered. "You're absolutely right. I asked you the other night if you were always so stubborn, and you told me you were often worse. This is worse. There's no way you can dig out all these lines. Give this section a few days to melt."

She'd been fine until he touched her. Actually, it wasn't the touching part she minded. It was the way he dropped his hand now that he had her attention that threatened the oddly tight hold she had on herself. Or maybe it was his suggestion that she do what she knew she never could that put the knot of anxiety in her chest.

"You can stop if you want. You can *go* if you want," she insisted, apparently not holding together anywhere near as well as she'd thought. "I can't."

It wasn't just the daunting work in this section of the sugar bush getting to her. Or even the biting cold. From the force behind her words, the frustration in them, he had the feeling the past few days were finally catching up with her.

Despite what she'd said about it being all right, he knew she was upset with the talk taking place over dinner tables even now about her father. More important, he knew she was struggling with the image she'd have of her dad and the possibility that she had a half sibling out there somewhere.

Then there was him.

There had been a time when she would have given anything to have him leave. He had the feeling from her accusation moments ago, that maybe she wasn't so anxious to have that happen now.

He didn't care to consider how he felt about that little revelation. He didn't want to question too closely why he hadn't left that day, either. At least, not beyond the fact that she'd needed the help.

"I'm not going in without you," he told her. "And you *can* stop."

Catching her by the shoulders, he stepped in front of her, his snowshoes bumping hers. Beneath his hands, it felt almost as if she were bracing herself. Against what in particular he had no idea. He just knew it would be foolish to stay out there working on a case of frostbite when the return for their energy would be so small.

The thought that small steps led to bigger ones and that she probably had to think in such terms to keep from totally overwhelming herself jerked hard as he closed his arms around her.

"At least for tonight. It's dark. It's freezing. And Rudy needs out," he reminded her, strengthening his case. "Come on," he murmured, feeling her stiffness reluctantly ease as he held her as close as the layers between them would allow. Touching her like this didn't count. He couldn't feel skin or shape anywhere.

What he could feel was the fight drain out of her as she finally rested her forehead against his chest, and the shiver that told him she was far colder than she was about to admit. He touched his gloved hand to the back of her hair, dipped his head to see if he could see her face.

"You okay down there?"

Lifting her head, she gave him a reluctant nod.

"I'm fine," she said, though she honestly wasn't sure what she felt just then. She didn't want to figure it out, either. It felt too much like something she didn't want to know. "I just need to check the tank and see if we have to boil."

She thought she heard him sigh a moment before he backed up and turned her around, aiming her for the top of the hill. Or maybe that small tired sound had been hers. She wasn't sure about that, either. She just knew that she had never in her life hoped that there wouldn't be any sap in the tank.

She almost wished it now.

If *almost wishes* counted, hers came true. The tank held little more than it had at that time last night. Considering that she'd wound up with less than a quarter of her usual production, it hardly seemed worth the effort to start everything up and clean all the equipment afterward.

The good news was that her power was back on.

Following the golden glow of lights to her house, she let Rudy out and started pulling off her gloves while trying to think of what she could heat up for supper. She needed to feed Rudy, too. He would be back in in a minute, pawing at his empty dish, and Jack had to be starving himself. If she focused only on the practical, she really would be fine. At least, she would if she could just shake the odd frustration competing with the fatigue she was trying not to think about, either.

Jack came in behind her, stamping snow from his boots and blowing on his hands after he pulled off his stocking cap and gloves.

"If you could be anywhere in the world right now," he asked, over the ripping sound of the Velcro tabs, "where would you be?"

Still working on her first glove while he hung up his parka, she didn't even hesitate. "In a hot shower."

"I was thinking more along the lines of Barbados, Hawaii, or Arizona in July when it's 110 and feels so hot a person can barely breathe. But a shower works.

"And if you could have anything right now," he continued, now working on his boot laces, "what would that be?"

"Anything?"

"Anything."

Watching him rise to toe off his heavy boots, she felt herself struggling with a wish list she wouldn't have imagined allowing herself to have less than a week ago. At the top of that list was that she badly wished he didn't have to leave. Right below that came the wish that he would hold her again. Really hold her. The way he had in the hall when he'd kissed her and made her feel so…much.

"That dinner would magically appear," she said, because he did have to go, and indulging such thoughts only made her want them more.

Shivering again, she dropped the glove she'd finally tugged off. With a sigh, she bent to retrieve it. It was her own fault she was so cold. She should have put on her parka sooner. She should have worn warmer gloves to dig in the snow. She should have worn a muffler, a stocking cap. She should have left well enough alone and come down off the hill when Charlie had left. Or, better yet, maybe she should have done what Jack had suggested she do and decided to wait for spring to melt the whole mess.

Her stiff fingers had barely touched the glove when it disappeared. Certain it was only weariness making her feel so discouraged, she straightened to see Jack holding it as he reach for her other hand.

As if he'd rather not watch her struggle, he eased off the other glove and tossed both of them onto the drier. "Then go get a shower and warm up." Reaching for her again, he pushed her parka back from her shoulders. "I'll wait for Rudy."

Trying to help, she tugged at her sleeve. "I know there isn't much out there, but I should boil first."

"That sap's not going anywhere, Emmy." Giving her a look of supreme patience, he pulled her sleeves from her arms himself and hung her jacket two pegs down from his. "Go take a shower. Get warm." He turned back to her to carefully slip away the wide fleece headband that had more or less protected her ears. "I'll heat up what was left from last night. Then, if you want, we can go start round two."

Emmy blinked at the top of his dark mussed hair. He'd just crouched to untie her boots.

"Jack, I can do this."

"Lift," he said, ignoring her, and grasped her calf to lift her foot himself.

The motion had her bracing her hand against his broad shoulder. She kept it there while he pulled off first one boot, then the other and rose to start working on the snaps of her vest.

It was then that she realized what she was seeing in his wind-chapped features. It wasn't impatience. It was simply concentration. It etched the lines deeper at the corners of his eyes. Tightened the corners of his mouth.

It had been so long since Emmy had been cared for that she had almost forgotten how it felt. But that's what Jack was doing. Taking care of her.

The realization squeezed hard at her heart.

"You're cold, too."

"Yeah," he conceded, working on a snap two down from her neck, "but I'm bigger than you are." He had more body mass than she did, more muscle to generate heat, more muscle to hang on to it. "That wind up there probably blew right through you."

The scratching at the back door had him glancing over his shoulder. "Hang on, Rudy," he called, and left her to let in her dog.

Rudy loped in, eyes bright, and rounded on Jack to be petted. "Hey, boy," Jack murmured, indulging him in the seconds before the dog rounded again to see if his dish had been filled.

A small frown creased his forehead when he looked back to where Emmy still stood. She hadn't moved. "What?" he asked.

She opened her mouth, closed it, shook her head. She couldn't believe how badly she wanted the feeling he'd just allowed her.

As he had in the sugar bush, he took her by the shoulders, turned her in the direction he wanted her to go. Their stocking feet were soundless on the pine floor as they headed into the kitchen that was bright with the lights that had been on when the power had died.

He moved her past the woodstove with its banked coals

and the electric range whose clock needed to be reset and veered her toward the doorway leading to the hallway to her room..

"Take your time," he said on the way. "Supper will be ready when you get out."

"You don't have to—"

"I know I don't," he cut in from behind her. "But you can use a break. Reheating isn't that big a deal, anyway."

Yes, it was, Emmy thought. She knew better than to think too far ahead. The most she ever allowed herself was a season. Maybe two if there was something she needed to plan for. But at that moment, as tired as she felt, as quietly, completely overwhelmed as she was at the thought of having to go back to the sugar house when she just wanted to get warm and not have to do anything for a while, he might as well have said he was having dinner flown in from the Ritz.

The weight of his hands on her shoulders eased when they reached the doorway. Shivering as the heat from the furnace started penetrating her clothes, or maybe from the loss of his touch, she crossed her arms over the chill inside her and glanced to where he stood waiting for her to head down the hall.

"I need to feed Rudy."

He caught her by the shoulders again. "I'll do it."

"He needs fresh water, too."

"Consider it done." One dark eyebrow arched. "Anything else?"

Certain from her hesitation that she had something else on her mind, he asked, "What is it?" Lifting one hand, he nudged a strand of hair from her cheek, carefully, because he didn't want his cold hands to hurt the cool skin of her face. "Just tell me and I'll take care of it."

The knot in her chest tightened with his touch. As she shook her head in incomprehension, the hair that had loosened from her listing, windblown ponytail fell over her cheek again. "Why are you doing this, Jack?"

"I told you." He eased the strand back again, just as gently. "Because I think you need a break."

"I mean, helping me in the sugar bush. You didn't have to stay today."

Her wide gray eyes held his, unblinking, intent. For a moment she was the little girl he'd last seen, looking at him as if trying hard to understand. But the impression vanished as soon as it formed and he found himself looking into the wise and weary eyes of a woman who touched him in ways he didn't understand, didn't totally trust and couldn't begin to explain.

He shouldn't be touching her. He especially shouldn't be wanting to back her toward her bathroom to get into that shower with her. But he was. And he did.

"Yeah," he murmured. "I did have to…. So." He spoke the word quietly, moving on before she could ask why he'd found it so necessary or before he could do anything he might regret. "Are you going to take that shower or not?"

For a moment Emmy said nothing. She simply stood there while he gave her a little half smile that did crazy things to her heart and his fingers absently massaged her shoulder.

She didn't know if he was aware of the small motion. All she knew for certain was that he was touching her, caring for her, caring about her—and that she really didn't want him to stop.

With the slow shake of her head, she replied with a quiet, "No."

The smile faded. "Why not?"

Because there's something I'd rather have than a shower, she thought, but simply didn't have the courage to say. Were she a braver woman, she would have. If she were more forward. More sophisticated. More whatever it was that she was not, she might have been able to tell this man who kept stealing pieces of her heart that she very much needed to be in his arms. Just for a little while.

Instead, she would settle for the next best thing. She would simply enjoy being with him for as long as he chose to stay.

Catching her by her chin when her glance fell, he tipped it back up. She didn't know if he'd sensed what had kept her from heading down the hall. Or if he'd recognized something he'd seen in her before, but he said nothing else. He just let his too-blue eyes slowly roam her face while her heart bumped her ribs and the funny ache inside her grew deeper.

He touched his fingertips to her cheek, his thumb to her lower lip.

"You know something, Emmy?"

The soft caress felt strangely warm. "I know," she said, since he'd mentioned it not that long ago. "I'm stubborn."

"That, too." He traced his thumb to the corner of her mouth, his eyes following the motion before he glanced up. "But I was thinking more along the lines of how you're never going to warm up just standing here."

She wanted to be held. Needed it, Jack imagined, considering how tightly wound she'd seemed to him since he'd found her on the hill. Lowering his hand, only then realizing how unconsciously he'd touched her, he eased his arms around her back.

Something squeezed inside him at the feel of her muscles beneath his touch. "You're shivering to your toes," he accused, focusing on the need for warmth. It was easier than thinking of the need he'd seen in her eyes. Or admitting that he needed to hold her simply because he couldn't stand not to.

"I'll thaw out in a minute," she finally said, her voice muffled. "How about you?"

With her hands clasped between them, her head tucked down and resting against his chest, he cupped his hand to the side of her face. There were fewer layers between them now than when he'd held her outside. Less fabric to mask how well her curvy little body fit in his arms. Even as aware of her as he was, he never would have imagined how good just holding a woman could feel.

"I'm fine where I am, too."

At his quiet admission, Emmy felt the tightness in her chest loosen a little more. It seemed easier to breathe when he held her. She had no idea why that was but she wouldn't question it now. Now, she wanted simply to…be.

"Jack?"

"Yeah?"

Beneath her ear she could hear the strong rhythm of his heart. Placing her palm over that steady beat, she moved closer to absorb the warmth seeping into her from his arms. "I'm going to miss you."

The beat didn't change, but his voice seemed to drop as he smoothed his hand the length of her ponytail.

"I guess that makes us even."

He murmured the words against the top of her hair, caught the scents of fresh air and herbal shampoo. Those scents moved into his lungs, entered his blood, worked their way to the hunger gathering low in his gut.

That hunger sharpened when she lifted her head and he found his mouth inches from hers. The warmth of their breath mingled between them as he watched her lips part and heard her slowly breathe in.

He could still remember the taste of her. He could still remember the little sound she'd made at the first touch of their lips.

Just once more, he thought. Just once. And lowered his mouth to hers.

Emmy couldn't help the small sigh that escaped from her throat. He drank in that small sound, gathering her closer as she moved closer herself.

They were there again. The feelings he'd made her feel before. Only they felt larger, somehow. Stronger. When he'd kissed her not far from where they stood now, she'd only been able to imagine what it would feel like to be cared for by him. Now she knew. She knew what it was to feel comforted and calmed, and to not feel alone. His warmth was there, too. As he angled her head, drawing her deeper into his kiss, she could feel it again, moving through her, into her, taking away the chill that had nothing to do with the goose bumps on her skin.

Needing more of that warmth, she skimmed her hands over the solid wall of his chest, slipped them around his neck. The shivers coursing through her seemed to change quality at the feel of his hard body molded to hers. Or maybe what altered the little tremors was the feel of Jack's hand slipping between them to pop open the last two snaps on her vest. Those fastenings had barely given way before he skimmed his hand between the sides of the quilted fabric to shape her waist, her ribs, the side of her breast.

Jack's hand went still a moment before he eased it from where it had drifted and forced it to the small of her back. Letting it drift a little farther, he pressed her closer, and swallowed the incredibly sweet taste of her along with his groan. The feel of her stomach pressed against the bulge behind his zipper was even harder to take than teasing himself with thoughts of how her breast would feel in his hand. It would fit perfectly, he was sure. She would fit him everywhere.

The certainty did nothing to ease the raw hunger clawing inside him. It did nothing, either, for the resolve that had already bit the dust about keeping his hands to himself. But he wasn't into analyzing system failures at the moment. He was too busy fighting protectiveness and pure physical need.

He'd never simply touched a woman and wanted her. And what he wanted now, he was better off not considering at all. It would also be a whole lot easier not to think about if he just went back to holding her.

Slowly lifting his head, he drew her hands from the back of his neck and held them against his thundering heart.

Emmy felt his chest expand with the deep breath he drew. She knew what he was going to do. He'd done it the last time he'd eased her away from him like this. He was going to tell her he needed to stop before he changed his mind about behaving, and that was the last thing in the world she wanted.

"For what it's worth," she murmured, her voice thready with longings she couldn't begin to define, "I wouldn't mind if you don't want to behave yourself."

The carved lines of his face were already beautifully taut, his eyes dark. As his eyes collided with hers it seemed that they went darker still.

The raw need in his expression nearly robbed her breath. That same desire lingered in his touch when he slowly traced the shape of her jaw. "You wouldn't say that if you knew what I was thinking."

It was that need that allowed her the boldness that had escaped her before. She could feel it in him as surely as she could feel the yearnings deep inside herself. "And what's that?"

"How badly I want you."

She tipped her head, echoing what he'd admitted before. "Then, I guess that makes us even."

The heat in his eyes turned to warning.

"I mean *want* you, Emmy. As in naked. And in bed."

His bluntness had barely caused her heart to jerk when she felt his hands settle at her waist. He apparently wasn't a man who allowed room for misunderstanding. "I understand *want*," she quietly assured him. She swallowed. Hard. "That's what I want, too."

She felt his fingers tighten, each pad seeming to burn through flannel and cotton a moment before he reached to slowly slip away the scrunchee holding her ponytail at its leeward list. That bit of gathered fabric had barely landed on the hallway table beside them before he threaded his fingers through her hair.

Letting the wind-tousled locks tumble over his hands,

he framed her face with his palms. Without a word he searched her eyes. He was giving her a chance to change her mind.

Her only response was to touch her fingers to his chest as she rose to meet his lips. His was to kiss her back, a little fiercely, and edge her toward her room while he worked at the buttons of her flannel shirt and tugged it from her jeans.

The hall was dim, lit only by the light filtering in from the kitchen. It reached as far as her doorway, spilling into her room in a pale slash across the foot of her bed and leaving the rest of the space in a deep sort of twilight.

Lost in the heat stealing the cold from inside her, she felt her knees bump the back of the bed. Jack pulled away long enough to grab his sweater between his shoulder blades, drag it over his head and tug back her quilts.

"You're going to get colder before you get warmer," he warned, sending her flannel shirt the way of her sweater.

She would have reminded him that he would, too, as she pulled the hems of his turtleneck and undershirt from the waistband of his jeans, but he was kissing her again. Her mouth. The corners of her eyes. Behind her ear. She kissed him back, playing an erotic game of follow the leader as they worked off turtlenecks and denims, then tumbled under the blankets to work on what was left.

Emmy had never ached before. Not the way she did when, barriers gone, Jack pulled her against his long hard body. Heat intensified everywhere they touched, that delicious warmth flowing between them, taking away the shivers and drawing her closer as his mouth took tantalizing little forays down her neck, to the hollow at the base of her throat, her shoulders.

She had never craved a man's touch before. But she did now as he trailed kisses across her collarbone and down to tease one breast. He touched her as if she were something exquisite, something precious. He made her feel that way, too, when he carried his kiss back to her mouth and, shaping her body to his, whispered that she was beautiful.

She told him he was, too. He chuckled against her mouth at that, then taught her the exquisite frustration of not being able to explore his body as intimately as he touched hers because he insisted that if she touched him the way she wanted to, he wouldn't last long at all. He saw no need to rush.

It was then that she realized she'd never felt passion. Never known raw aching need. She knew it now. Yet, even as he created yearnings she never knew existed, what mattered to her most was that she felt safe with him. Secure for that moment. And that moment was all she cared about.

All Jack cared about was that his hold on his control had grown from taut to paper thin.

He couldn't believe how beautifully Emmy responded to him. Or how incredible her small, soft body felt against his harder rougher one. There was a fragility about her that belied the supple, athletic strength of her muscles, and a gentle femininity that was driving him quietly insane.

He had known want before. He'd just never felt need. The need to please a woman, to take care of her, to protect her, possess her. What Emmy thought and felt mattered to him. Her struggles left him torn between admiration and compassion. But mostly, he'd never felt the kind of need gripping him at the feel of her small, soft hands stripping away those last precious bits of control. The kind he felt when the demands of his body caved in to the desire boiling his blood and he eased himself over her.

He gritted his teeth at the exquisite feel of her rising to meet him. That need burned in a place he hadn't known existed. A place she had somehow found and claimed and that was coming to feel as essential to his existence as his next breath. Even more demanding was the need to claim her right back.

That realization should have shaken him to his core. And it would have had it not been for the feel of her when he slipped into her warmth, and the mind-numbing sensations that no longer allowed him to think at all.

Jack didn't realize they had fallen asleep until he heard the tick of something metal near the bed. Emmy had heard it, too, and was already lifting her head from his shoulder.

In the dim light he saw her push her hair from her eyes and smile at Rudy. The dog stood at the side of the bed, his tail slowly wagging and the license tab on his collar bumping the aluminum dish in his mouth.

"You want to be fed, sweetie?" he heard her ask.

He skimmed his hand over her bare hip, need stirring once more. "Are you talking to him or me?"

"Both of you," she murmured, reaching across him to tousle Rudy's fur.

Catching her by the waist, he buried his face in the silk falling over her shoulders, nuzzled the side of her neck. "Good," he murmured. He felt her shiver, heard her sigh. "Then we can get that shower."

Chapter Eleven

Emmy hadn't heard Jack slip from her bed, but she could hear him talking to Rudy as she headed down the hall in the blue fleece and denim she'd pulled on before a quick encounter with her hair- and toothbrushes. It sounded as if they were discussing something her little would-be hunter had nearly caught outside a few minutes ago. Jack was wanting to know what Rudy would have done with the hapless critter had he managed to snag it.

She couldn't help the small smile that formed. Hearing him eased that sudden disquiet she'd felt when she'd wakened to find him gone from her bed. Hearing the smile in his voice eased it even more. She didn't know when Jack would choose to leave. She didn't know when she would have to deal with the sense of loss waiting to be felt. But she wasn't going to ruin the time she had with him worrying about it. He was there now.

Memories of the hours she'd shared in his arms had her heart beating a little too quickly as she turned into the kitchen and came to a silent stop. Jack crouched near the mudroom door. Having already been outside, he was dressed and wearing his heavy hiking boots. Rudy sat on his haunches in front of him, totally focused on the dog biscuit in Jack's hand and his tail moving like a windshield wiper across the floor.

Man and her precious little beast had clearly bonded.

The biscuit disappeared a moment before Jack rose. She didn't know if he'd heard her or simply sensed her presence. But when he turned and his eyes settled on hers, Emmy felt her smile slowly slip away.

It was then that she noticed he had already shaved and that his hair looked damp from a more-recent shower than the one they'd taken together after they'd made supper last night. Mostly, she noticed the caution etched deeply in his expression as he walked over to where she stood rooted to the floor.

With aching familiarity, he slipped his fingers through her hair and tipped her face to his.

"Morning."

"Morning," she echoed, and closed her eyes as his head descended.

He kissed her thoroughly, completely, altering her heart rate and her breathing and reminding her of the steam they'd created in her shower before they'd tumbled back to bed. Yet, as desired as she felt in his arms, as safe and protected, she felt as if she were holding her breath once more when he lifted his head to slowly scan her face.

He looked as if he were memorizing her. Or trying to figure out what to say.

That sense of impending loss returned with a vengeance. He was leaving. She knew that as surely as the north wind blew. She just didn't want to hear it. Not yet.

"I should start breakfast," she said, and with a smile that felt very brave, ducked away to fill the carafe on the coffeemaker. He would need to eat, and she suddenly, desperately, needed something to do.

She reached into the cupboard, pulled down flour and baking powder, then remembered the coffee and turned to dump grounds into a filter.

Jack watched her uneasily. Seeing that she wasn't using the enamel pot she had on the woodstove now that the power was back, he picked up the carafe she'd started to fill and filled it himself.

If not for the strained quality of her smile when she thanked him for that, he might have thought it were any other morning and she was just hurrying to get them fed and to work. She seemed agitated though. She also looked as if she were trying very hard to hide it.

He appreciated the feeling. He felt a little unsettled himself.

He'd thought when he'd arrived in Maple Mountain that he could take care of business and walk away. But his business wasn't finished. The property he'd intended to return was still in his name, and he had no intention of leaving it that way. Then there was the disturbing fact that Emmy had more work on her hands than she could possibly handle. Charlie had told him it would take him and Emmy two weeks to repair and rerun the downed and damaged lines.

And that was in addition to whatever sugaring they'd be able to do in the evenings.

Tired of the mental pacing he'd done since he'd wakened, he moved to where Emmy had just set a mixing bowl covered with orange poppies on the counter. He'd intended to tell her last night that he was leaving this morning. But that had been before her need to be held had taken priority and rational thought had eventually evaporated. It had also been his intention to talk to her again about taking the property that was beginning to feel like an albatross around his neck—even though the last thing he'd wanted to do was leave with her upset with him.

Taking her by the shoulders, he turned her around—and glimpsed the vulnerability that had always touched something deep inside him.

"Emmy," he began, smoothing her hair, "I have to leave in a while. But I'm coming back." He spoke quickly, making the decision even as he caught her chin to keep her from looking away. He had no idea how he would manage that. He just knew that he would. The same sense of responsibility he'd felt to return the land made it impossible now to leave her with all that damage. She'd already lost part of her production. The longer it took to repair her lines, the more she would lose.

Then there was that nagging sense of need he felt toward her. That need to be there for her. He felt certain, though, that once he made sure she was taken care of, that need would no longer be there.

"It'll be the end of next week at the earliest, but you can tell Charlie not to try bringing any big branches down himself."

The tension he'd felt in her shoulders had leaked out like air from a bicycle tire. "You're coming back?"

The smile in her eyes nearly undid him. He'd never seen her smile like that before. It seemed to light her from within, and made him wish he didn't have so little time before he had to go. But because he did have to leave—and soon—he made himself fasten the top button of her fleece shirt when he really would have rather unbuttoned them all. "Boston's closer than New York," he told her, which pared the trip down to about four hours one way. "But I'll only be able to stay for a couple of days."

Emmy didn't care how short his stay would be. He would be back. At that moment, nothing else mattered. "That's okay," she said, swallowing past the tiny bubble of hope pressing under her heart. She touched her fingers to his chest, watched the guard slip from his eyes. "It's just good to know I don't have to say goodbye forever right now."

Goodbye forever.

Jack felt his brow pinch at the phrase.

"No," he murmured. Caving in to the pull of her beautiful smile, he lowered his head to hers as the distant rumble of Charlie's snowmobile joined the hum of the fridge and the gurgle of the coffeemaker. "We only have to say goodbye for now."

The morning Jack had left, Charlie had come in to have coffee with him while he'd had his breakfast. Her die-hard old friend and part-time employee had thought to get an early start on the day, and had been sorely disappointed to learn that Jack was leaving, but he seemed almost as heartened as Emmy felt knowing that Jack would be coming back to help. He'd told his friend Amos that, too. Who'd told Smiley, the postman, who had mentioned it to Claire, the mayor's gossipy wife, who had told everyone else.

Emmy suspected that was why Agnes seemed to pay particular attention to the items she chose from her shelves a week later, and why the clearly curious woman kept looking at her as if there were something she wanted to ask but didn't care to with another customer in the store. Bertie stood two aisles over, pinching the loaves of bread the bakery truck had delivered the day before to make sure they still felt fresh, and stewing over whether she should buy dried prunes or canned.

Emmy's inclination was to tell the woman Mary referred to as a cranky old sourpuss to buy both.

"So, Emmy," Agnes called from her perch behind the counter, "you have how many acres runnin' now?"

"Only eight," she called back from the section of the cooler holding produce and dairy products. Her attention shifted from the sap line she was having trouble finding, because so many other sugarers were also ordering it, to the head of lettuce and semigreen hothouse tomatoes that pretty much accounted for Maple Mountain's fresh produce this time of year. She ached for her summer garden. "I hear the Henleys and the Bruners are back to full production."

"Good thing, too. We need the sugar houses for the festival. Folks would be mighty disappointed to come see syrup being made and find there's no one boilin'. 'Course those families have all those teenagers and in-laws to help 'em out," she qualified, eyeing the package of dried spaghetti Emmy had set next to butter, eggs and milk on the counter. "But you've got help comin' here pretty soon, too."

There was a leading edge to that statement. Knowing that Jack would be mentioned sooner or later, surprised it had actually taken two full minutes for the subject of him to come up, Emmy chose the greener of the dozen heads, passed on the tomatoes in favor of what she'd put up herself last summer and, grabbing a bag of potatoes and one of apples, carried the last of her purchases to the front of the store.

Bertie had decided on canned.

"You really think he's comin'?" Pulling a folded bill from the pocket of her heavy canvas jacket, the woman with the short electrified hair framing her thin face eyed Emmy's purchases herself. "Or did he just say that because it was the polite thing to do?"

Tactful, the woman was not.

Emmy did her level best to keep her anticipation out of her voice. "He said this morning that he was." Jack had called just before seven o'clock, wanting to catch her before she went into the sugar bush. He would be there in the morning, which was the only reason she wasn't in the bush with Charlie now. "Since he said so, I'm sure he will be."

Agnes, wearing the crested-wren-nesting sweater she'd knitted herself, offered a faint and speculative smile. "So you really don't mind him being around? Other than for his help, I mean?"

So that's what she wanted to know, Emmy thought, preoccupied. "He's a nice man, Agnes. And no," she admitted, wondering what she was forgetting to buy, "I don't mind him being around." She didn't know if she should put on a pot of spaghetti sauce to simmer for dinner tomorrow night, or make something more elaborate like beef bourguignonne. Either one could simmer all day while they worked, but she wanted dinner to be something special.

She decided on the beef, which meant she needed to get up earlier in the morning because preparation would take longer.

She was barely getting any sleep now as it was.

"Do you have fresh garlic?"

"Only powdered." Agnes wasn't about to budge from her subject. "How long is he stayin'?"

"Just a couple of days. He has to be on Hilton Head Monday morning. No, that's Tuesday." A thoughtful frown touched her brow as she tried to remember what he'd said about his schedule after she'd asked if he'd caught up with his work. He hadn't, which was why he had a dinner meeting tonight that prevented him from leaving Boston any earlier. "Monday is Providence. He has projects in both places."

"Well, I must say," Agnes replied, finally starting to ring up Bertie's purchases since she'd reached the counter first, "it surely seems he went on to make somethin' of himself. Of course, I sort of suspected that when he showed up here lookin' like somethin' out of an L.L.Bean catalogue," she confided, putting prunes in Bertie's drawstring market bag. "Never would have imagined it when his family left here." Her tone dropped as she reached to ring up the loaf of freshly-squeezed bread. "All things considered, it seems I might have done a little misjudgin' where he's concerned."

The confession was cautious at best. It could take forever for old notions to give way to new in and around Maple Mountain. Considering that Agnes's change of heart had taken place in only a couple of weeks, the admission had nearly come with the speed of light.

If the woman beside Emmy were ever to change her mind, her exasperatingly critical attitude would keep anyone from ever knowing it.

"Well, I still think it's dreadful that he let the cat out of the bag about her father after all this time. I can only imagine how that had to make her feel," she insisted to Agnes, totally overlooking how she might be making Emmy feel simply by bringing up the subject, much less talking as if she weren't there. "If he is coming back to help, I imagine it's because he feels guilty about having done that, right along with his father takin' that property. I'd say that man definitely owes her."

Agnes had the grace to look guilty herself. No one would have known about Emmy's father had she not mentioned what she'd overheard.

"I imagine he does feel a little that way," she agreed, adding the bread to the bag, ringing up the total. "If he didn't, he'd have never come to give her that property back in the first place. But it's possible he's coming back now just because he's a nice man," she defended for Emmy. "Just like Emmy said."

Bertie was as tall as Agnes was not. Looking down the point of her nose, something she couldn't help, given the foot difference in their heights, her mouth pursed.

"I still say he owes her."

"I didn't say he doesn't."

"He doesn't owe me anything," Emmy insisted, wanting them both to stop. Agnes was arguing in her favor. So was Bertie, for that matter, hard as it was to grasp that at times. Yet it didn't feel as if they were doing her any favor at all. "He's coming back to help because he's…a friend," she quickly decided to call him. "He certainly doesn't owe Charlie anything and he's coming to help him, too."

"Of course, he is."

Supportive of her as always, Agnes offered a smile, then hit the total button on the old-fashioned cash register, its ping joining the chime of the bell as the door opened. The middle McNeff girl walked in carrying her mother's grocery list.

"So," Agnes continued, while Emmy wiggled her fingers at the twelve-year-old and the girl smiled and wiggled back, "what are you fixing him for supper?"

Losing interest in the direction of the conversation, Bertie picked up her bag and headed for the door. Anxious to be going herself, Emmy told Agnes she wasn't sure yet and turned her attention to tracking down garlic powder, since she couldn't remember just then if she had any at home and didn't have time to come back.

The thought that Jack owed her in some way had never entered her mind before. It had never occurred to her to blame him for word getting out about her father, either. Word that had finally proven itself to be true.

She'd discovered that undeniable fact three nights ago when she'd been boiling alone and decided to try to find the spot where her dad might have stashed a bottle. While poking around the sugar house, searching out every conceivable nook and cranny, she'd found a loose floor plank that was nearly always covered with boxes. Under it had been a half-empty bottle of whisky, and the paper he'd signed giving up his right to Baby Girl Jones.

She hadn't been sure of what all she'd felt as she'd stared at the copy of her father's scrawled signature. Just as she wasn't sure what she felt now at the possibility that Jack might be coming back out of a sense of duty. She hated that Bertie had so thoughtlessly planted the idea that Agnes had unwittingly reinforced. Yet, the possibility that Jack's reasons for returning were far different from hers for wanting him there took root like a weed in the spring and simply refused to die.

Jack had no business leaving Boston that weekend. He'd either stayed late at the office or had business dinners every night for the past week. He hadn't even been in town Tuesday and Wednesday. He'd spent that time in meetings in New York before he'd flown back Wednesday night in time to finish reviewing contracts for a meeting at seven the next morning.

He hadn't had a chance to unpack much of anything, much less take the time to make sure that all his possessions had arrived. To get to his bedroom, he literally wound his way through the maze of boxes and furniture that blocked the view of the bay. His assistant, bless her extremely efficient heart, had interviewed housekeepers for him, but he hadn't even had time to talk to the three candidates on the list she'd handed him yesterday. He had, however, found the boxes containing his sheets and towels, so he'd been able to make his bed. He had no idea where his comforter was, however. Or the wardrobe containing the other half of his suits. At least the one he'd found had held some of his winter ones and his overcoats.

He'd hit the ground running that morning, too. His

alarm had gone off at three-thirty. He'd been showered, packed and out the door by four. It hadn't been until he'd pulled through the Starbucks four blocks down from his new condo and hit the expressway that he switched gears from mentally going through how productive his dinner meeting had been last night to wondering if Emmy had been able to get more line. He knew she'd been running low when he'd left.

He'd been thinking of that off and on all week. And of Emmy. Thoughts of her had crept constantly into his consciousness. But it was at night that those thoughts wreaked their worst havoc. The remembered feel of her ruined his sleep and filled him with a restless ache that had him abandoning the effort and burying himself in business journals until exhaustion took over and allowed the rest he craved.

That fatigue was already draining away when he pulled into her plowed driveway a little after eight o'clock that morning. It was the last thing on his mind when she opened her back door to him and he saw her welcoming smile.

Rudy greeted him first. His new-found friend seemed more interested in being out in the brilliant sunshine, however, than in sticking around for more than a cursory pet. With a bark and leap, he headed out to run a lap through the snow that looked to Jack as if it had melted considerably since he'd left.

With Emmy waiting, he reached for the edge of the storm door she held for him. She was dressed for the sugar bush. Brown denims, beige turtleneck, heavy black-and-brown-plaid shirt. It was her soft smile he noticed most, though, and the strain behind it.

Assuming the strain came from working all day and half

the night, he considered doing what he'd thought about every night since he'd left and pulling her into his arms. She stepped back before he could, though, and motioned him in.

As if afraid he might miss something, Rudy bounded back, snow clinging to his paws, and shot past the doors before Jack could close them.

"How did your meeting go last night?" he heard Emmy ask on their way into the kitchen.

"It went great. We're bringing the interior designer on board." Leaving his jacket on its peg, he followed the sway of her high auburn ponytail. Her hair shone in the familiar room's overhead lights, seeming to tease him with the appeal of its softness. "And the lighting people. The way things are moving, the project might even finish ahead of schedule."

His glance moved from her slender back to the room that seemed even brighter and cozier than he'd remembered. Something tantalizing was already simmering somewhere. Inside the oven, he guessed, since its light was on. Two thermoses sat on counter, apparently filled and ready to go.

A thin sheet of paper lay by the refilled fruit bowl on the long pine parson's table. He'd barely noticed it when its distinctive format snagged his attention and had him glancing at it again. He couldn't see what it said from where he stood in the middle of the room, but he recognized it as a legal document. The sort filed with the courts.

"Is Charlie coming this morning?" he asked.

"Actually, he left for home a while ago. He came to help sugar last night, so he was up late," she explained, wishing her defenses hadn't made her move from him so quickly. She wanted so badly for him to hold her. Almost as badly as she wanted him to tell her that she was worrying for nothing, that he was there because he wanted to be. "He can either sugar or work in the bush during the day, but I'm afraid he'll run himself down doing both."

Picking up the thermoses, she turned to put them in the backpack in the mudroom. Jack stood ten feet behind her.

He was dressed much as he'd been before. The same heavy hiking boots, denims that looked a little newer than the last pair he'd worn and a thermal sweater, in a shade of blue this time, that did incredible things for his eyes.

His focus wasn't on her, though. He was frowning at the paper on the table.

Realizing what had his attention, she eased the thermoses back onto the counter. She'd left the document there on purpose. She wasn't totally sure why, but once the initial shock of having found it had worn off, one of her first thoughts had been to show it to him.

"I found that in the sugar house."

With all the work to be done, she had thought she would share it with him after they returned that evening. Since it had his attention, and since she desperately wanted her ease back with him, she headed for it now.

The onionskin paper had been folded twice and kept in the yellowing envelope now lying beneath it. The corners of both the envelope and the page were water stained and both had been damp when she'd found them. The type looked as if it might have faded, too. But that could have been because what she had was obviously a copy of the original. Still, the words were easy enough to read.

The faint smell of must met her nostrils when she handed the sheet to him. He took it, his expression quizzical in the moments before he realized what the document was.

With his dark head lowered, he scanned the few lines below the State of Vermont court heading, and the line below that read In the matter of the adoption of Baby Girl Jones. Releasing a quiet hiss of air, he looked to where she silently watched him.

Thinking it no wonder she seemed a little uneasy, Jack set the paper back on the envelope.

She now knew for certain about her father's infidelity, and that her parents' relationship wasn't what she'd thought it to be. She also knew that somewhere out there she had a half sister her father had allowed to be put up for adoption.

"Do you want to find her?"

"I don't know. I think so. I mean, I'd like to," she qualified, clearly vacillating, "but I don't know what her situation is."

"What do you mean?"

"Maybe she's never been told she's adopted."

"Then talk to the adoptive parents first," he suggested, wondering at the selflessness of her mental struggle. She'd found family. Because she had no relatives to speak of, and knowing what the family she'd once had meant to her, he didn't doubt for a minute that she would love to have that relationship. Yet, her concern was with not wanting to upset the other woman's life.

Probably, he figured, because she knew so well what personal upheaval was like herself.

"Do you want me to help you locate them?"

His offer drew the delicate arches of her eyebrows inward. "You'd do that?"

He looked as if he couldn't believe she'd asked such a thing. "Of course I would, Emmy. I have friends who are lawyers. I'll talk to one of them when I get back."

"I can't afford a lawyer."

"I can. Let me take care of this, okay? It's the least I can do."

It took a moment, but as his claim echoed in her head, Emmy could feel her gratitude for his thoughtfulness slide straight to the uncertainty over his actions she simply couldn't shake.

Turning to the table, hating the doubts, she picked up the document to put it back in its envelope.

"You don't have to do anything for me, Jack," she said, her tone surprisingly casual. "You're doing more than enough coming back to help." The paper crackled lightly. "You know you didn't have to do that."

"And you know I couldn't leave you with all that extra work," he replied, touching her shoulder.

Her glance slid to his. "Why not?"

For a moment he looked as if he couldn't believe she'd asked that, either. Apparently, he thought his reasoning should be obvious. "Because I know how hard it is for you to get help."

It wasn't like her to confront. It wasn't her nature to challenge. And the last thing she wanted to do was push him into a corner if the apprehension she felt was just her insecurity bracing her to lose someone else she'd cared about. But she'd fallen in love with him, and she badly needed to know that it wasn't obligation he felt toward her most.

"I mean why couldn't you do it?"

The little furrows between his eyes deepened an instant before his hand slipped away.

"Is it because you feel you should?" she asked, when his only reply was hesitation. "Because of what happened between our fathers?"

The furrows deepened. So did his silence.

"I know you felt a sense of responsibility to come here the first time," she told him, torn between wishing he'd tell her to be quiet and not allowing herself to back down. Now that the opportunity had presented itself, she also needed to let him know that any responsibility he felt truly wasn't necessary. Burdening him with her little crises was the last thing she wanted to do.

"And I know you feel bad about all that's happened around here with my family. It took me a while, but I'm dealing okay with all that now." She'd resigned herself to it all, anyway. "I just don't want you to think you have to be here because you feel it's your duty."

She glanced down at the yellowed envelope she held, slowly set it back on the table. "I have the feeling that's why Dad stayed around. Because he'd felt obligated and guilty. And that he owed his wife and daughter.

"The more I've thought about it," she confided, needing him to know what else she'd realized, "the easier it's been to see that his drinking was probably a way to numb himself to the mess he'd made of everything. I still believe his death was an accident." She had to. Her father had loved her. He would never have left her on purpose. "But I think his drinking had impaired his judgment and that his problems had been more on his mind than his driving when he'd slid off the road."

Crossing her arms beneath the little ache Jack's silence put in her heart, she blinked at the unmoving wall of his chest. He'd been right. She had been protected. And she probably had only seen what she'd wanted to see. She'd tended to do that a lot over the years. "I imagine the reason I never heard them argue was because they never really talked," she continued, refusing to wear those protective blinders any longer. "I'd just been too young and naive to notice that they'd been miserable."

She tipped her head, met the disturbing disquiet in his eyes.

"I don't want you to feel any of that where I'm concerned. A sense of duty, I mean. Or guilt," she added, because it was looking more by the minute as if both were possibilities. "So I really hope that isn't why you're here."

And please tell me why you are. And where we're going. Or if we're going anywhere at all.

The ache seemed to deepen a bit as he looked away.

It grew deeper still when he opened his mouth, closed it again and planted his hands on his hips.

Jack couldn't look into her eyes and lie. There was no way he could deny the obligation or sense of responsibility he felt toward her. They had been there since the day he'd arrived. He couldn't deny the protectiveness he felt toward her, either, or the physical desire he'd truly never felt for any other woman. He just had no idea which outweighed the other, or if that desire was only clouding his judgment where she was concerned.

Considering that he should be in Providence at that very moment, going through the partially constructed facility he was meeting about on Monday, the latter was a distinct possibility.

"I told you why I'm here," he said quietly.

He knew she wanted more than that. He also knew he was totally unprepared to answer the questions he could swear he saw in her beautiful gray eyes. He'd never considered what his return might mean to her. He'd thought only to help her get back into operation and get the other property into her name. Then he'd felt certain his need to be there for her would be satisfied, and his obligations there met.

"I meant what I said about getting you an attorney to help you find whoever adopted your half sister," he said, moving back to what had somehow led them to this suddenly uncomfortable place. "Have you learned anything that might help with that?"

He doubted a change of subject had ever been so artless. But Emmy had the grace, or maybe it was the sense of self-protection, to allow it.

"I haven't," she admitted, tightening her hold on herself. It had been duty that had brought him back. By denying nothing, he'd as much as admitted that he was there because he felt bad about all that had happened, and bad for her for having to go through it. He cared for her because he felt sympathy for her. And that meant he didn't care for her at all the way she did about him. "I really haven't had time."

"So what are you going to do now?"

She could tell from the way he glanced to the envelope then back to her that he wanted to know who she might ask to find out who her father's lover might have been. Common as the name was, she knew of no Jones in the area. It could have been a generic name to protect the mother, for all she knew. But she didn't want to think about that now.

She couldn't. She was too busy fighting the awful suspicion that beyond feeling obligated to her, he'd felt sorry for her. Worse, that he'd felt sorry for her when he'd held her, when they'd made love.

Her sense of self-preservation had been sorely lacking where he'd been concerned. It kicked in now as she backed away.

"I'll do what I always do." Six feet of pine flooring now separated them. It might as well have been a mile. "The rest of this sugaring season will mostly be a loss, but I'll get through and get by."

Needing to hide how she hurt, she offered a smile. "In the meantime, you shouldn't waste your time on me. I'm fine, Jack. I really am. I'm actually a lot like you. You're the only other person I know who doesn't seem to want anything but your work. Somehow it seems to be all you need. I just need to remember I don't need anything but work, either."

Jack had no idea what to say just then. He could practically see her withdrawing, could almost physically feel it. The phenomenon was as disconcerting as the little voice telling him he should feel relieved, that he could get back to his hustling and not worry about the responsibility he felt for her anymore. She was letting him off the hook. She'd just told him he owed her nothing, that the problems between their families were settled.

He had never intended for their relationship to get complicated. And it wouldn't have, he reminded himself, had he kept his hands to himself. But somewhere along the line, he'd become sidetracked by her spirit, her gentleness, the feel of her against him, and he'd totally lost focus of his original goal.

That goal had been to offer an apology and return property. Those had been his sole intentions when he returned to Maple Mountain two weeks ago. Yet, at that moment, dealing with the unresolved part of that situation held no importance at all. He wasn't sure if it was his ego or his heart that felt sucker punched. He wasn't even totally sure why the feeling was there. All he knew for certain was that it was time to step back and regroup.

"Do you want me to leave?" he asked, at loss for where else to go from there.

Her smile was gone. So was the strength from her voice. "It might be best."

As if he hadn't fully expected that, one corner of his mouth pinched before he gave her a little nod.

Just like that, Emmy thought. Just like that the hope she should have never allowed herself to feel was gone.

Her aching heart seemed to be battering her ribs as he walked up to her and lifted his hand to her face.

"Since Charlie won't be around to work today, I could at least help you until dark."

She shook her head, needing him go.

He seemed to realize that as his mouth thinned again. "Then, promise me something?"

Swallowing past the knot in her throat, she said, "Sure."

"Promise me you'll take care of yourself?"

"Only if you promise me back."

The pads of his fingers drifted to her jaw. "Deal."

"Deal," she repeated and, wanting to be brave, rose on tiptoe to kiss his cheek.

Her lips had barely touched his recently shaved skin and his clean scent tightened the ache inside when she pulled back. As she did, she felt the hand that had settled with such familiarity on her shoulder give a little squeeze.

"Do yourself a favor, Emmy," he said, reluctantly letting that hand fall. "I know you love this place. Just don't bury yourself here. Okay?"

He didn't wait for a response. He turned then, leaving her hugging herself while he crouched in front of Rudy, told her dog to keep an eye on her and after ruffling the fur on her blissfully oblivious pet's head, headed for the mudroom and his jacket.

Long moments passed before she heard the back door open and the quiet, almost hesitant thud of it closing behind him. That decidedly final sound seemed to echo long after his car pulled from her drive.

Chapter Twelve

Maple Sugar Days in mid-April had once been Emmy's favorite celebration. People came for miles to attend the Saturday-morning pancake breakfast, to watch candy-making demonstrations and visit the craft booths filled with everything from specialty foods to beautiful, hand-crafted furniture of bird's-eye maple and quilts appliquéd with maple leaves. The area's sugar houses opened their doors. And the women's league put on a chicken dinner and the sugar-on-snow party that drew every local for miles.

Depending on Mother Nature's mood, snow could still be heavy on the ground when festival weekend rolled around, the roads could be visible for the first time in months, or the snow could be gone and Northern Vermont knee deep in mud season. When the festival arrived this year, Emmy thought the weather perfect. Bare patches exposed the dead leaves around the trees, and a few hardy crocus peeked through the remaining snow on her flower beds. The days were clear and cool. The nights clear and colder.

For years the Larkin sugar house had welcomed the visitors who came to see syrup being made. And over those years, traditions had evolved in the little family operation that had become inviolate as far as she was concerned.

When she'd been a young girl, her mother had kept a pot of cider spiced with cinnamon warm on the hot plate in the sugar house for those guests. And her father, who spent most of his time at the evaporator feeding the fire, stirring the syrup and keeping the curious from getting close enough to burn themselves on hot metal or steam, would bring out the red and gold maple leaves he'd collected and pressed the previous fall.

Emmy's job had been to hand out those brilliant bits of autumn foliage to the children and to help her mom serve the cider that had been pressed from their own apple trees.

Even after her father's death, when she and her mom had done the sugaring themselves and there had been no time to make the little maple candies, maple cream and maple sugar that had been her mother's specialties, their sugar house had been on the Maple Sugar Days tour and the cider and the leaves had been passed out.

Emmy had faithfully kept those traditions. Until now. The tubing she'd ordered had arrived, but not in time to increase her production before the festival. She was only getting enough sap for one boil an evening.

She stood in her bedroom, holding up two white blouses on hangers. One had a high neck, the other a collar.

Turning to where Rudy lay chewing on the oval of plush pink that had once been a bunny but now resembled a football with an ear, she held one in front of her, then the other.

"What do you think, Rudy? It'll be under a sweater, so high collar? Open?"

Rudy lifted his eyes, the remaining body part in his mouth and the rest dangling, and went back to chewing.

"That's what I thought, too," she murmured, and returned both to her closet.

Threading her fingers through her hair, she backed up and plopped down on the foot of her bed.

She couldn't believe she was having trouble deciding what to wear that night. Since her sugar house wouldn't be open for tours, she'd offered to help out at the community center and serve sugar on snow, the maple treat northern New Englanders craved. But she didn't have to be there until four that afternoon.

It was barely after nine o'clock in the morning now.

She should have been in the sugar bush. She actually should have been out there an hour ago. She'd just been too busy procrastinating. For the past half hour, anyway. She hadn't wanted to call Jack before then and possibly wake him up—if he was even home.

Knowing she would only drive herself crazy sitting there, she hauled herself up and down the hall. He had given her his phone numbers before he'd left the first time. All four of them: main office, private line, home and cell phone.

For days she'd been working her way up to making the call. She'd actually decided last night that it was time. It was actually past time, she admitted, picking up the receiver and making herself punch in the number for his home phone.

The ringing on the other end began immediately, causing her heart to jump and her courage to falter.

There hadn't been a day go by that she hadn't missed Jack and wished he were by her side. Or a night that she hadn't realized how futile it was to try to pretend nothing about her life had changed. She went through the same motions she would have before he'd appeared and upended her life, but nothing about her life was the same. She hadn't meant for it to happen, hadn't even realized it was until it had been too late. But because of him, she had started to dream of things she'd been afraid to let herself think about, of maybe someday having a husband, children—and a life away from the only one she'd ever known and had fought so hard to protect.

But that peace had cracked and shattered when Jack had left, and she had no idea how to get it back.

When she heard his phone ring the third time, she almost breathed a sigh of relief. She would get his answering machine. It would be better that way, she thought. She could just leave a message asking her question, and he could leave a message for her, answering it.

The line clicked a moment before she heard a deep "Hello?"

The painfully familiar voice wasn't recorded.

"Hi," she said, and sat down at her desk because her knees suddenly felt a little shaky.

"Emmy."

Jack unzipped the jacket of his jogging suit and tossed his keys onto the credenza inside his foyer. Had the caller ID on the cordless phone there not indicated that the call was coming from Vermont, he would have let the answering machine pick it up while he grabbed a towel and dried off. The mist he'd started jogging in an hour ago had turned to steady rain along about his fourth mile.

It was also about then that he'd decided he was never going to get her out of his mind.

His heart rate still slowing, he spoke the first thought to enter his head at the sound of her voice. "Are you all right?"

"I'm fine," came her quiet reply. "I'll only keep you for a minute," she continued, sounding as if she thought she might be bothering him. "I just wondered if you'd give me the name of the real estate person you used when you bought that parcel of property."

That property had been on his mind that morning, too. Everything about her had. But then, there hadn't been a day go by that thoughts of her hadn't haunted him. "You don't need her to get that land," he said, thinking that was what she wanted, wondering what had finally made her change her mind. "I'll just give you the deed." If you'll give me your name, he would have added, but she was already talking.

"That's not why I called," she quietly told him. "I want to sell what I already have. The land. The sugar house. My home. You're the only person I know who's dealt with a real estate agent. The people I know around here don't tend to sell their property. They pass it on to family."

He'd started for his bathroom, since it was the nearest place with a towel, and passed the spacious living room that his new housekeeper had finally cleared and arranged. Even with its floor-to-ceiling view of the bay, the room with its sleek modern furnishings seemed sterile to him. It needed color, heavier fabrics. Warmth.

He now came to a dead stop in the hall.

"You want to sell everything?"

"As soon as I can."

In the two weeks since he'd walked away from her, he had picked up the phone a dozen times to see how she was doing. And a dozen times he'd hung up because he'd told himself he needed to stop worrying about her. She'd survived this long without him; she would be fine.

He wished now that he had called. She wasn't fine at all. He knew how emotionally bonded she was to her home and her land. He knew, too, that she'd never known a life other than the one she lived on that land in Maple Mountain.

"Why do you want to do that?" he asked, his protective instincts clearly in place. "Is it because the sugaring is so bad? If you need money—"

"It's not that."

"Then what is it?"

The line hummed with her hesitation.

"Emmy?"

"It's because of what you said before you left," she finally replied. "You said I should do myself a favor and not bury myself here." She gave a little laugh, the sound clearly intended to make light of her discovery. It failed miserably. "I just didn't realize until after you'd gone that I already had."

He didn't care at all for the hollowness in her voice. He didn't care, either, that he hadn't had time to come to grips with what he'd began to realize about her while running in the rain. He could deal with it on the way to Maple Mountain.

"Hey, listen," he said, his tone casual despite the odd urgency he felt. "Why don't we talk about this? I need to run by the office for a couple of hours. But I can be there by five. Six at the latest."

"You don't need to come here, Jack. Really," she softly stressed. "I don't want to intrude on your time. I just need the name of your real estate agent."

Ignoring her protest, he headed into his bathroom, grabbed a towel to wipe over his face and moved into his bedroom to change. "You'll be down from the sugar bush by then. Right?"

"Jack…"

"Emmy," he echoed. "I'm coming, okay? Where will you be?"

"At the community center," she finally told him. "It's Maple Sugar Days this weekend. I'm serving there tonight."

Jack had forgotten how many people came out for what was actually a celebration of spring in the north country. The melting fields and piles of snow that lined the now-bare two-lane road through Maple Mountain gave way to trucks and cars parked headlamp to taillight when he turned onto the short road that ended at the brightly lit community center. On the other side of Main Road behind him, the lane to the little community church was packed, too.

So was the utilitarian white building itself when, having finally found a place to park, he walked through its front door and was greeted by the din of locals and visitors sitting elbow to elbow at eight-foot-long tables.

The walls of the wide, high-ceilinged room were lined with craft booths and hundreds of construction-paper maple leaves hung suspended from the rafters. He remembered making leaves like that himself. All the grade school kids had. Still did, from the looks of it, he thought, and glanced over the crowd for Emmy.

The conversations near him seemed to quiet.

The one taking place two tables ahead of him stopped completely.

For a quick, uncomfortable second, he thought of the cool receptions he'd been greeted with before by some of the locals. But he had no time to do more than notice a few people's heads moving together to whisper to each other before he heard a familiar, "Hey, Jack!"

Charlie waved a half-eaten doughnut. From the table beyond him, Joe lifted his hand, too.

Jack waved back as Hanna Talbot walked in front of him with a large jar of home-canned pickles. "You home for the festival?" she asked on her way by.

He hadn't seen Hanna since he'd checked into her family's hotel the night before the storm. Her naturally reserved smile seemed infinitely more friendly than it had been then.

Smiling back, he said he was, since it seemed an easy enough way to explain his presence, and let his glance sweep back across the room.

Several of the local women moved between the tables carrying baskets of biscuits and maple bread and platters of fried chicken. Others were serving the dessert of sugar-on-snow that was really the reason everyone was there. The sugar of pure, thick and hot maple syrup had been drizzled like lacework over snow packed in aluminum pie plates. The chewy confection was greeted with ready forks and smiles and followed with a bite of pickle or donut from the bowls and plates in the middles of the tables.

Passing baskets of biscuits, Mary Moorehouse lifted her chin at him and smiled. A couple dozen feet closer, the wiry, outspoken woman he recognized as Bertie Buell narrowly eyed his casual brown leather jacket and heavy ivory sweater.

Lips thinned, she motioned him over to where she sat at a table with the minister and his wife.

"If you're lookin' for Emmy, she just went into the kitchen," she said, and took a bite of pickle.

He'd barely offered a quick "Thanks" before he looked up to see Emmy returning with a tray of pie tins.

He caught her eye a moment before she turned to speak to the teenage girl beside her. Looking like a teenager herself, petite as she was, she handed the girl the tray and walked over to where he was now being watched by nearly all the locals and half the visitors.

Mindful of their audience, he kept his hands to himself as his glance skimmed the deep auburn hair she'd pulled back in a braid and the pine-green sweater that turned the silver chips in her gray eyes to slivers of pewter. He couldn't believe how much he'd missed her. Or how he hated the caution he saw in the delicate lines of her face.

"Can you get away?"

"I just need my coat."

The faint buzz of speculation joined the general chatter of conversation and laughter as they moved to the coatracks beside the front door. He would have taken her quilted black coat from her to help her slip it on had she not quickly pulled it on herself and headed for the door. She seemed as anxious as he was to escape the two hundred sets of eyes glued to their backs.

The warmth and once-familiar scents gave way to the crisp night air. In the merging halos of lights flanking the door, he saw her look up a heartbeat before that glance shied away.

"It really wasn't necessary for you to drive all the way up here, Jack."

"I'd have been back sooner or later. What do you want to do?" he asked, skirting past that little admission. "Do you have to go back in there, or do want me to follow you home?"

"I should go back in." Still looking cautious, or maybe it was self-protective, she pushed her hands into her coat pockets. Her breath trailed off in a fog. "Let's just walk."

Pushing his hands into his pockets, too, mostly to keep from reaching for her, he moved with her past the parked trucks and cars before they angled toward the quarter mile of snowfield separating the center from the back road that led to the old mill.

Here, away from the lights, the thinned layer of snow glowed blue in the brightness of the nearly full sugar moon.

"Do you want to tell me what's going on?" he finally asked.

"I told you on the phone. I want to sell everything."

"You're not serious, are you?"

She didn't hesitate. "I've never been more serious in my life."

Emmy really wished he'd listened to her and stayed in Boston. She didn't believe for a minute that he was there for the reasons she needed him to be. Seeing him had also just neatly undone whatever negligible bit of progress she'd thought she'd made toward getting over him and moving on.

Since moving on is what she knew she had to do, the last

thing she needed was him trying to talk her out of it. And he would. She could tell from the disbelief in his voice.

"I don't want to stay here," she told him, when what she truly didn't want was to continue on as she was. She just didn't know any other way to avoid it. "I'd always lived with the idea that I had to preserve what my parents had struggled to keep intact. I think somehow I thought I'd be letting them both down if I didn't keep the house and carry on the sugaring business and the Larkin's Products name. What they'd left me was all I had," she admitted, over the quiet crunch of snow beneath their feet, "so I didn't let myself think of wanting anything else.

"But living alone from one season to the next isn't how I want to spend the rest of my life," she insisted. "Unless I want to bury myself out there forever, I need to find something more, Jack. Like you did. So, please," she asked, would have begged if she'd had to. "Don't try to talk me into staying."

In the pale moonlight, she watched him glance toward her and braced herself for his arguments. She was sure he had them. He'd had plenty when he'd tried to talk her into taking the parcel of property that now belonged to him, whether he liked the idea or not.

"Okay, then," he agreed, a little too easily it seemed. "But how about some options?"

"To leaving?"

"To selling. I really don't think that's something you should do," he said, telling her exactly what she'd expected to hear. "Unless you sell it to me."

That, she had not anticipated.

"Why would you want it?"

"So I can hold it for you." As Jack had thought about what she wanted during his four-hour drive, it had occurred to him that buying it himself was the most logical thing to do if she were truly serious. And he really hadn't doubted that she was. As practical and sensible as he knew her to be, Emmy wasn't a woman to make such a decision lightly. "I know you want to sell it, but I have the feeling you would eventually regret having let it go. If I buy it, then you can buy it back anytime you want. Or you can come back whenever you feel the need."

There wasn't a doubt in his mind that she would miss her home. She might not miss the work, the worry or the weather that could wreak havoc on her life and her livelihood. But she would miss her house and her land. And Maple Mountain. It was too much a part of her. Just like this place was a part of him. Despite the bad memories, being back even for a while had made him appreciate the uniqueness of where he'd grown up himself. It would be good to come back to the country, to work the land. Once in a while.

"You would live there?"

"I'm not in a position to do that," he told her, because he would miss the city even more. "Or, rather than sell it," he suggested, because he'd thought about this, too, "you could keep it all and have Charlie and his wife move in while you're gone. I know he'd like to be out of his son's house. His wife would, too." The old guy had confided that himself. Grumbled it somewhat wistfully, actually. "You know he would be right at home taking care of the sugar bush. He could do your sugaring for you, too. He told me his grandson will be old enough next year to help out. And

I guess Mary used to work with him when they had their maple farm."

In the shadows, Emmy studied the lines of his noble profile. His offer to buy her land and hold it for her had been incredibly kind. Incredibly generous. But then, she knew he was a kind and generous man. He'd been proving that since the first day he'd arrived.

She also knew that the offer he'd so easily made had been possible because of what had happened between their fathers.

I didn't want to have to worry about hanging on to every penny I had, he'd told her. *I wanted to have enough that if a friend got himself into trouble and needed help, I could give him what he needed and not worry about whether I ever got it back.*

A friend, she thought. Even though she strongly suspected it was his sense of duty driving him, that was what he was trying to be.

As much as she wanted that friendship and as good a friend as he would make, she ached for so much more.

More.

It was as if he'd taught her the word.

"I would love to give it to Charlie and Mary." She honestly couldn't imagine anyone she'd rather see there. "It's just that I need the money from the sale to start over somewhere else."

"Where would you go?"

A cloud slipped across the moon, dimming its glow as they walked next to each other across the field. "I'd like to go to design school," she told him, because confiding in him had come so easily. "Some of the best ones are in New York, but I can't see taking Rudy there."

Jack couldn't see her energetic little canine there, either. Or her, for that matter. Not straight from Maple Mountain. But it wasn't thoughts of her alone in the city that suddenly had him dealing with a totally unfamiliar sense of uncertainty. They had just edged up to the reason he'd had to see her.

"What about Boston? That's where you'd intended to go when you gave up your scholarship."

"I know." She had thought about that, too. It had been her first choice, actually.

But that's where he was.

Emmy hunched her shoulders against the cold air, her focus on the gleam of the moon on the snow now that the moon was back. She knew Boston was a big city. She knew the chances of running into him would be roughly equivalent to her stick-straight hair suddenly turning curly, but she'd know he was there. And then she'd never get over him.

Her silence pushed him on.

"If you were there, it would be easier for us to see each other." The caution he'd sensed in her now filled him. "I'll go wherever I have to, Emmy. But it really would be easier if we were at least in the same state."

Emmy came to a dead halt at the side of the road.

Despite her best efforts, that intrepid bubble of hope had resurrected itself when he'd said he was coming. It now jammed itself squarely in her chest.

It also prevented her from saying a thing when he stepped in front of her and slowly scanned her face. She'd never seem him look so hesitant, or sound so certain.

"A really wise friend said something I haven't been able to forget," he told her, hoping the stunned look in her eyes was a good thing. He'd once thought her reserved. Yet the woman now seemed totally artless, nearly incapable of hiding her responses. At least, around him. "He said that a man can't be happy having nothing to do, any more than he can be happy having nothing to do but work."

She tipped her head, her eyes luminous in the pale light. "That sounds like Charlie."

"It was."

He threaded his fingers through his hair. He'd never laid himself on the line before. Not his heart, anyway.

"I know you don't want me to feel a sense of obligation toward you. Or responsibly. Or duty. But I do. Not because of our fathers," he insisted. Doing what he'd done so many times before, he caught her cheek with his palm, turned her face back to him when she looked away. "But because those are just part of caring about someone. I know I'm not doing the best job of telling you all this. I mean, this whole thing sort of blindsided me. But I want more than my work," he finally said, because that was the bottom line.

She seemed to have frozen in the snow. He edged closer, traced the shape of her bottom lip with his thumb.

"I want you, Emmy. Actually, I need you," he admitted, because he hadn't felt whole since he walked out her door. "I know you need more than what you have, too. And I know that what we had together was good," he continued. "If you're willing to give me another chance, maybe between the two of us we can figure out how to find a little balance in both of our lives."

He wanted evenings by the fire with Rudy curled up beside them while she studied and he waded through whatever work he'd had to bring home. He wanted coffee with her in the morning before they had to rush out the door.

What he wanted more than anything was to wake up with her in his arms and to know that she was there for him, and for her to know he was there for her.

"I think we can make this work…" he murmured, feeling relief wash through him as she stood quietly absorbing his touch "…if there's any chance you can love me, too."

From somewhere beneath her heart, Emmy felt the bubble break free. Behind it, realization filled the void that had lived inside her for so long. Love him, too, he'd said.

Her hand felt as if it were trembling as she rested her palm on his chest, felt the strong beat of his heart. She couldn't help the smile curving her mouth.

"I think we can make it work, too." She hadn't just found more. She'd found it all. "And I already do."

Jack finally had what he'd hoped for. Her smile. The one that seemed to make her glow from inside and radiated the warmth that touched him in a place he hadn't known existed.

She loved him. The thought seemed incredible as he hooked his arms around her waist and drew her slender body against his. Almost as incredible as the fact that he'd had to come home to Maple Mountain to find the part of himself he hadn't even known was missing.

"I love you," he murmured, his breath warm on her cheek.

"I love you more."

She whispered the words as she looped her arms around his neck, flowing into his kiss, kissing him back with the same longing she felt in him. There was wonder in that kiss, too. And promise. And hope. There was also enough heat to have her knees feeling a little weak when, long moments later, a pair of headlights illuminated them right where they stood.

Jack lifted his head. Emmy turned hers to glance toward the SUV that had practically slowed to a stop as it passed them.

It was Agnes.

There wasn't a doubt in Emmy's mind where the talkative woman was headed, or what would happen once she got there. In less than a minute, half of the people in the community center would know for sure what half the town had already begun to suspect. Stan Larkin's daughter had fallen hard for Ed Travers's son.

"This is going to be interesting," Jack muttered when the vehicle's lights disappeared.

"What will?"

"Going back in there."

"Actually, I don't have to. My shift was over when you arrived."

He grinned. "Good," he muttered, and pressed a quick kiss to her lips. When he lifted his head, his smile had turned to curiosity. "So," he said, flatly. "Maybe now you'll tell me?"

"Tell you what?"

"Your name. You never have told me what it is."

She tipped her chin, shrugged as if the matter were of no consequence at all. "It's just Emily."

"No middle name?"

"None."

"Just Emily. I like that," he told her, cupping her face with his hand. "But I think I'd like Emily Larkin-Travers better." One dark eyebrow arched. "Any chance you could get used to the sound of that someday?"

Emmy felt as if her heart were about to burst as she met the smile in Jack's eyes.

He was the man who had let her dare to dream, to want,

to finally put the past behind her. She couldn't think of anything more healing to that past than the blending of their names, either. But she was thinking more of the future and all it held with him in it when she raised up to meet his kiss—and told him she'd never heard anything more wonderful in all her life.

* * * * *

Don't miss the last instalment of the
GOING HOME *series.*
Confessions of a Small Town Girl
is out in August 2006.

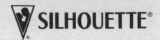

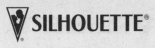

♥ SILHOUETTE®

0606/23b

SPECIAL EDITION™

PRESCRIPTION: LOVE by Pamela Toth

Montana

When city slicker Zoe Hart arrived in Thunder Canyon, she wasn't expecting sexy local physician Christopher Taylor to sweep her off her feet the way he did. But would Zoe opt to stay with the man who made her pulse race like no other?

THE OTHER SIDE OF PARADISE
by Laurie Paige

Seven Devils

There's an instant attraction between Mary McHale and her new boss, Jonah Lanigan, but Mary's eerie similarity to the Daltons who live on the next ranch takes her away. She must decide whether to stay with her new-found family or follow her heart...

FAMILY MERGER by Leigh Greenwood

Millionaire Ron Egan's teenage daughter was pregnant and beautiful Kathryn Roper seemed to be the only bridge between Ron and his daughter. But should Kathryn and Ron ignore their powerful yearnings for each other...?

Don't miss out!
On sale from 16th June 2006

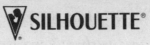

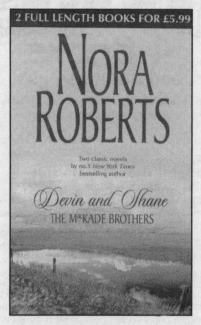

FREE!

4 Books
and a surprise gift!

We would like to take this opportunity to thank you for reading this Silhouette® book by offering you the chance to take FOUR more specially selected titles from the Special Edition™ series absolutely FREE! We're also making this offer to introduce you to the benefits of the Reader Service™—

- ★ **FREE home delivery**
- ★ **FREE gifts and competitions**
- ★ **FREE monthly Newsletter**
- ★ **Exclusive Reader Service offers**
- ★ **Books available before they're in the shops**

Accepting these FREE books and gift places you under no obligation to buy, you may cancel at any time, even after receiving your free shipment. Simply complete your details below and return the entire page to the address below. You don't even need a stamp!

YES! Please send me 4 free Special Edition books and a surprise gift. I understand that unless you hear from me, I will receive 6 superb new titles every month for just £3.10 each, postage and packing free. I am under no obligation to purchase any books and may cancel my subscription at any time. The free books and gift will be mine to keep in any case.

E6ZEF

Ms/Mrs/Miss/Mr ....Initials...............................
                                                    BLOCK CAPITALS PLEASE
Surname...
Address..

....
....Postcode ....

Send this whole page to:
UK: FREEPOST CN81, Croydon, CR9 3WZ